Uprising

Uprising

Gateway Series Book 3

Brian Dorsey

Chapter 1

Muffled voices and shapeless forms pervaded Paladin Emily Martin's thoughts as she struggled for consciousness. Coming out of her haze, she strained to open her eyes against the light in the room.

"She's moving," she heard a woman's voice declare. "Get the doctor."

Martin's eyes opened and closed again against the brightness of the light above her bed.

Then the pain hit as a lightning bolt of agony shot through her left arm and into her spine, causing her to moan.

"Can you hear me, Paladin?"

Martin opened her eyes again, focusing on a tall, thin woman wearing the uniform of a Humani medical officer.

"Paladin Martin?"

"Yes," she grumbled. "Where —" Another bolt of pain shot through her body.

"We'll get you some more meds," assured the woman. "The regeneration process can be very painful."

Her clarity renewed by the pain radiating from her arm, Martin flashed back to her last memories. She went back to the realization that her planet's elite were using her and the other inhabitants as pawns to maintain power and appease their Xen masters. After finding out the truth, she'd hunted down Tyler Stone, her former commander whom she had been tricked into believing was a traitor. After finding Stone and confirming his innocence, she agreed to return to Alpha Humana to help obtain access codes that would allow the Terillians to conduct undetected jumps through the Dark Zone and into Humani territory. The jump access would allow the Terillians to carry out a massive three-pronged attack against the Humani. If successful, the attacks would destroy the Gateway Station as well as ProConsul Astra Varus's secret base on Dolus, where she was developing a genetic weapon and building a private army she planned to unleash on both her allies and enemies alike. And finally, Alpha Humana itself would be attacked in an attempt to ignite an insurrection against ProConsul Astra Varus and the First Family Elites.

"How long?" huffed Martin.

"Ma'am?"

"How long have I … have I been out?"

"I don't know exactly, Paladin," replied the nurse. "But you've been here six standard weeks, and it took them a few weeks to get you home when they found you. What do you remember?"

Martin paused before she answered. She remembered everything — the meeting on the Terillian ship and the plan for a simultaneous attack on the secret base at Dolus, the Gateway Station, and Alpha Humana itself. The searing pain in her left arm reminded her of the beating she took at the hands of her former commander's lover, Terillian Major Mori Skye, in order to promote the lie that they had escaped; she even let that bitch cut off her hand just to sell the story.

"The Traitor …" She knew Stone was no traitor, but she had to play her part. "He must have freed himself." She shook her head, feigning frustration. "They tried to take the ship."

"How frightening," gasped the nurse.

Martin noticed a camera high on the wall over the nurse's shoulder. She had an audience.

"Did they get away?" asked the nurse.

The woman in front of her may have actually been a nurse, but Martin recognized a well-planned interrogation when she saw one.

"How should I fucking know?" shot back Martin. "I put a round into the Traitor after he took my fucking hand." Martin grunted against the pain as she pushed her torso off the bed. Staring into the nurse's eyes, she continued. "But at least two of them are dead," she said, her gaze shifting from the nurse toward the camera. "If ProConsul Varus would like to know more, maybe she can come ask me herself."

"Excuse me?" asked the nurse, her face growing red.

"Are you even a real nurse?" asked Martin.

"That will be enough, Nurse Chan," said another woman entering the room. She was older and wore the uniform of a Humani officer.

Martin squinted, trying to read the name on her blouse, but the medication was still clouding her vision.

"My name is Colonel Valaria Travarus, Paladin Martin," said the woman. "I am your doctor."

"And you work for the ProConsul," added Martin.

"We all work for the ProConsul, Paladin," retorted the colonel as she began to scan through Martin's medical files.

"Of course," said Martin with a smile, "but I have a feeling your line of communication is a little more, uh, direct than others."

"As is yours, Paladin."

"Well, then perhaps maybe we should both speak with her," said Martin. "Now."

"Soon, Paladin," said the doctor, her face devoid of emotion. "And yes, you have been watched. After you were found in the escape pod and the debris of the transport was found nearby, there have been a lot of questions."

"Well if someone wants answers, maybe they should just ask me," replied Martin. "Are you intelligence?"

"No, Paladin. I'm the ProConsul's personal physician."

"No shit," replied Martin.

"Uh, yes," said Colonel Travarus, breaking her stoicism in reaction to Martin's bluntness. "There are questions, but you have served the ProConsul with bravery and clearly sacrificed," added the doctor as she glanced toward Martin's left arm.

"Can it be fixed?" asked Martin as she looked down at a large, metallic cylinder attached to her left forearm. It covered the area where her hand had once been.

"Yes, Paladin. But the initial growth stage for a new appendage is very painful. That is why you were kept unconscious until now."

"How much longer until —"

"Another month in the growth chamber, then two more getting strength and dexterity."

"I will get full strength back?"

"You should, but we won't know for sure until you have to start using it."

"Okay," Martin replied as she exhaled and swung her legs off the side of the hospital bed. The movement sent pain racing again through her arm.

"You shouldn't move just yet," replied Travarus. "The —"

"There's nothing wrong with my legs, right?" asked Martin as she pulled a medical tube from her arm.

"Well, no," answered Travarus, "but the pain will be almost unbearable without meds."

"Then give me a pill or an injection, but I need to be on my feet."

"Even if we give you an injection, if you're conscious, you are going to hurt."

"I'm used to pain," said Martin as she looked down to see a small pool of blood on the floor trickling from where her IV had been. "Can you put some coagulate on this before I bleed to death?"

"Of course," said Travarus, reaching for a small applicator. "You'll heal faster if you rest," she added as she applied the sticky gel to Martin's arm.

"If I rest, I get soft," replied Martin. "And my mission isn't finished."

"Well, that is between you and the ProConsul, Paladin Martin. But for now it is most definitely on pause."

"Hmm," replied Martin. "I need to see the ProConsul."

"In due —"

"Colonel," interrupted Martin, "I want to see Astra Varus today. And unless you think I am any less dangerous with only one arm, I suggest you get one of those Praetorians that I know are waiting outside that door and have them tell the ProConsul I will see her today."

***

Martin, with a Praetorian guard at each side, stood in the otherwise empty receiving chamber of ProConsul Astra Varus. Her arm pulsed with pain, but she wouldn't let that stop her. She needed to look the ProConsul in the eyes and make sure her cover wasn't blown. Astra was cautious — and ruthless; the sooner she could convince the ProConsul of her loyalty, the better.

"So you let the Traitor get away," said the Praetorian to her right.

"Screw you," she replied.

"Pretty fucking convenient," replied the other.

Martin mechanically turned toward the second Praetorian.

"Does this look fucking convenient?" she asked through her teeth, holding the regeneration canister on her hand to his face.

The Praetorian returned her stare. "If you weren't the ProConsul's little pet project —"

"You wanna dance, Praetorian?" she interrupted with a smile. "I don't need both hands to —"

"I see your attitude is still intact, Paladin Martin," interrupted Astra Varus as she entered the room.

Martin and the two Praetorians snapped to attention.

Martin watched as the ProConsul strolled toward her chair. *Just get there and sit down already,* thought Martin.

"So, Paladin," mused Astra, settling into her chair. "What is so important that it draws you out of recovery and me from … well, anything I was doing?" Astra leaned forward in her chair. Martin saw the ProConsul's normal expressionless face transition, her rage barely contained behind a chiseled smile. "I would think after your utter failure on your last mission you might not want to see me, or even return to your people."

Martin took in deep breath. More than ever, the desire to drive her sword into Astra's black heart burned at her. But she must play her part. "I did fail my people … failed you." She almost choked on the words. "But I needed to report to you and request permission to go back after him as soon as I am able."

"None of which would be necessary if you had not failed me!" shouted Astra, her anger boiling over as she rose from her chair and stepped toward Martin.

"You are right," replied Martin, still at attention.

"Look at me!" shouted Astra. "Look at me so I can see the shame of failure in your eyes!"

Martin shifted her gaze toward Astra, now only a meter from her. "As you wish,

ProConsul." She only hoped hatred would also pass for regret.

Luckily, it did.

"Well at least your failure has brought you a little humility," said Astra, her expression less severe. "But tell me why I should give you another chance."

"There is no one …" Martin stepped toward Astra. "… no one on this planet that wants to see those who turned against our people brought to justice more than me," she replied, returning Astra's gaze. She could see Astra's hatred for Stone radiating from her very being. "And there is no one else with the skill to do it."

She stared at Astra, trying to glean some inkling as to the ProConsul's thoughts.

"Well, Paladin," replied Astra, "there are questions about what happened."

"And I have the answers."

"Very well, then," said Astra as she turned and ascended the steps to her chair. "Enlighten me," she added.

"The Traitor must have broken free of his bindings and let the others loose —"

"Who were the others?"

"There was a smuggler pilot and what I can assume was an engineer … and this other Ter …" Martin paused. She needed to convince Astra she knew nothing, but wanted to see the ProConsul sweat a little. "She looked similar to the bulletins on the Traitor's whore but was different. Her features … almost reminded me of a wolf, but very muted. It was like nothing —"

"A wolf?" asked Astra, her posture stiffening in her chair. "Are you sure?"

"Yes, ProConsul," replied Martin. "Almost like she had been genetically altered." She could see the apprehension on Astra's face. Now it was time to set the hook. "Looks like the Ters are experimenting with genetic hybrids."

Astra's expression eased. "Very interesting, Paladin," said the ProConsul. "You will need to pass this information onto Colonel Travarus so she can look into it."

"Shouldn't I speak with Intelligence?"

"No," shot back Astra. "That would be premature … the Colonel works directly for me and will inform the necessary people in Intelligence, if it is warranted."

"Of course, ProConsul." *That was fun,* thought Martin.

"Now back to your failed mission," said Astra.

Martin had hoped the little hint at her secret plans of genetic alteration had thrown Astra off her game. It didn't.

"Yes, ProConsul," she replied. "He must have let the others free. The damned engineer made it to the engine room and knocked us out of the jump sequence. From there it was four against one, which wouldn't have been a problem, except one of them was Stone."

"So you said in the hospital room you injured the Traitor?" asked Astra.

Martin knew she had been listening.

"The pilot and the engineer were no problem. And then I found Stone." She was making it all up, transferring her anger toward Astra and the First Families into her story. "We were fighting and then the other one, the altered one, hit me from behind. She distracted me, and the Traitor took my hand. I grabbed the woman's pistol as I fell and put a round into his torso. After that, I retreated to deal with my wound. I went after him again, but he and the woman jettisoned their escape pods. I was on my way to the cockpit to run them down when I noticed they had rigged the ship to blow." She let the hatred for Astra Varus and all like her flow through her, peaking her emotional response as she continued. "I had no choice but to evacuate the ship."

"Hmm," replied Astra to Martin's emotional report.

Martin glared at Astra, waiting for either acceptance or death. She was prepared for either.

"While it vexes me that you allowed him to escape," continued Astra, "your weapons were inventoried when you were rescued and your blade was found to have Terillian blood on it."

"All of my blades have Terillian blood on them," said Martin dryly. "But they haven't been soaked with the blood of the Traitor, or his whore," added Martin. "That's why I have come to ask to continue my hunt and to pick a team to assist me."

"You are asking for help?" asked Astra, her head tilted slightly. "How very unlike you."

"I can handle Stone, but if he's surrounded by Rangers, I'll need people to keep them busy."

"And how many will you need?"

"Their skill is more important than the number, ProConsul," replied Martin. "I request permission to interview candidates from all services, regardless of family status, to find my team." She turned toward the Praetorian to her left. "Including your Praetorians. Once they are chosen, we will leave as soon as I am ready."

"What if the Traitor just disappears in the time it will take you to heal? Why should I wait for you?"

"Tyler Stone will not simply disappear," laughed Martin. "We will hear of him, and when I'm ready, I will find him … and I *will* kill him." She stepped toward Astra. "And you can send as many people as you want after him." She smiled. "Because no one else can take him."

<h1 style="text-align:center">Chapter 2</h1>

"We've got to be faster," said Major — and honored Ka-itsenko — Mori Skye to her company commanders, her fierce green eyes betraying her frustration. "It took twelve minutes to make it from the breach to the control room. That's too slow."

Tyler Stone, now fluent in the Akota language, stepped forward. In the three standard months since they laid the initial plan for the attack on Alpha Humana, the Akota had taken the time and effort to build near full-size mockups of a Humani orbital destroyer and battlecruiser on the Akota home planet of Luta-tunkan. The ship mockups were only one of the many preparations for the massive attacks. If Martin was successful in her clandestine mission to alert First Family leaders who were resistant to the rule of Astra Varus and her Xennite masters, the invasion could spark a revolt and return control of Alpha Humana to the people instead of the oligarchy of First Families.

"Due to the heavier armor of Humani orbitaldestroyers near the engineering and weapons spaces, the boarding location closest to the reactor control room is the crew compartment. We need to be able to lock in, breach, and fight our way to the control room before the ship security forces or engineers realize our objective," said Stone.

"We have a great opportunity here thanks to Rickover's little invention and Magakisca's knowledge of Humani ship layouts," said Mori, using Stone's Akota name. "During the attack on Alpha Humana, the Scout Rangers assigned to Task Force Eagle will board as many orbital destroyers as we can. We will follow a diversionary assault with of regular forces which will attempt to board near the hangar bay locations. Once they are engaged and distracting the ship's security forces, we'll breach and get to the reactor control room as fast as we can."

"Once we're in, we'll access the control room itself and find the panels marked 'Master Protection System.' Each platoon will have ten of these little electronic boxes," said Stone, holding Rickover's invention in the air. "Just attach this box to the panel and flip this switch," he pointed. "The circuitry inside should override the signals in the Master Protection System and force the reactor to shut down."

"Are we sure this will actually work?" asked one of the company commanders.

Stone knew that when it came to engineering, Rickover didn't make mistakes. "It will work."

"Each platoon will be assigned a Humani orbital destroyer when the battle starts. Once the breach is made, two squads will move to the forward reactors and two will move aft," said Mori. "If we shut enough reactors down, we will prevent them from being able to bombard our landing zones on Alpha Humana from orbit. We might even be able to take down their propulsion and self-defense systems."

"Preventing these ships from turning their main batteries on our LZs will save thousands," added Stone. "But we have to be fast. If they find out what we are doing, they can override their safety systems and prevent us from shutting down their reactors."

"And that's why we are going to keep doing this until we can do it under eight minutes," said Mori. "Muster your troops and we'll run it again in thirty minutes."

Stone turned toward Mori as the company officers exited the mockup reactor control room. "Do you think it will actually work?"

"If they go for the first wave of regular troops. If we make it through their ship self-defense systems. If we can actually breach … and if Rickover's contraption works … I'd say fifty-fifty."

"So better than normal," said Stone with a smile.

"A lot better," laughed Mori.

"Ka-itsenko Ino'ka," announced a lieutenant as he entered the compartment, "please excuse the interruption, but I have been sent for Magakisca."

"I'm still training," replied Stone.

"Whoever it is will have to wait," added Mori, slinging her rifle over her shoulder.

"I'm sorry, Ka-itsenko Ino'ka," insisted the officer. "The Shirt-Wearers have requested a meeting with him."

Stone looked toward Mori. *What do the Shirt-Wearers want with me?* he thought. He could tell from the look on Mori's face that she had no idea either.

"Well, I guess we'd better go," said Mori, stepping toward the exit. "All company commanders —"

"Major, uh … Ka-itsenko Ino'ka," interrupted the officer again, "they asked for Magakisca alone."

"What?" asked Mori, her head tilted slightly and her brow furrowed.

"I don't know why, ma'am," replied the officer. "I was just sent by Shirt-Wearer River to bring Magakisca alone."

"I see," replied Mori.

Stone could tell she was as confused as he was. "I —"

"You should go," said Mori. "It must be important."

"We'll talk later," said Stone.

Mori nodded. "Yes."

"Okay, let's go," said Stone to the officer.

Exiting the mockup, Stone's eyes quickly adjusted to the brightness of the early afternoon starlight on Luta-tunkan. The fresh smell of evergreen trees and other flora filled his senses, reminding him of Sierra 7, or at least what it had been before the war charred its landscape. As he and the officer made their way to a nearby elevated platform, Stone wondered how many other worlds would suffer the same fate as Sierra 7 before this war was over.

A military hover car awaited them at the platform. Looking to distract himself from his own thoughts, he spoke. "So what is the protocol?"

"Protocol?" replied the officer. "I don't understand."

Stone had become very comfortable with the Akota language, but maybe he had said it wrong. "Protocol … the process of interaction with the Shirt-Wearers." He'd been with the Akota long enough to understand their concepts of military courtesy were completely different compared to the rigid Humani style he had known.

"There's no protocol, Magakisca. Just show proper respect toward an elder. Other than that, they're Akota … like the rest of us."

"Thank you, cousin," replied Stone.

"My name is Sa-Hanhepi."

"Lieutenant Red Moon," replied Stone, "what is your clan?" Stone was getting used to Akota small talk.

"I'm from the Big River Clan, here on Luta-tunkan."

"This planet is beautiful," said Stone.

And it was beautiful. Despite their technological advancements, the Akota seemed to have made a deliberate effort to stay as close to nature as possible. It showed in the way the planet's natural flora mixed with the architecture, including the elevated hoverways which left the surface to the plants, trees, and animals. Few areas were developed for wheeled vehicles, leaving mostly well-maintained pathways designed for minimal impact on the landscape.

"We decided long ago that advancement at the cost of the environment wasn't advancement," replied Red Moon. "But it does have its downside."

"What's that?"

"Numbers," replied Red Moon. "In order to support our natural growth, we have had to expand first to the other planets we now call our home planets, and then further into systems to create colonies. This process is slow and limits our natural growth, which in turn limits our military strength. We have even begun terraforming formerly uninhabitable worlds, at great expense, in order to enhance our carrying capacity while not overpopulating any one planet or colony."

"So that's why the Dark Zone planets' populations are so low."

"That, and years of decay," replied Red Moon with a hint of resentment. "Populations in all of our systems were low, even your … uh … I mean the Hanmani … I mean Humani —"

"Hanmani is fine," interjected Stone. He had grown use to his home planet being called Hanmani, coming to realize it wasn't the negative term he had once thought it was, but a term relating to the lost nature of his people.

"The Hanmani population was no different before the Xen captured it." The lieutenant paused, shaking his head. "Then generations later when they attacked us, their numbers were limitless. That one planet holds so many people."

Stone had never really thought about the numbers. His one planet, with its cramped megacities and strained resources, had faced dozens of Akota worlds.

"They do have some land that is still left to nature," replied Stone, "but that mostly belongs to the First Families or is utilized for agriculture or resource management," he added, immediately realizing he had negated the point of his original statement.

"Either way," replied Red Moon, "there has always seemed to be so many of them. It's almost like they were bred to fight us."

"They were," answered Stone, the reality of Alpha Humana's purpose weighing heavily on him.

"If the Great Spirit wills it, maybe the rest of the Hanmani will someday be reunited with their long-lost cousins."

"Perhaps," replied Stone, but he was lost in contemplation. The Humani had become so different from their ancestral relatives, the Akota. Maybe Emily Martin was right; they had become too different. Or maybe Mori was right and the reunification and assimilation of the Humani into Akota and greater Terillian culture was the right thing. But the right thing for whom? His head began to hurt.

"We're here, Magakisca," said Red Moon as the craft came to a stop.

The door slid open and Stone stepped onto the platform. Looking down, his heart skipped a beat as he saw the forest ground over fifty meters below. Catching his breath, he looked back toward a large set of wooden doors on the opposite end of the platform. Dark and bold, they had a massive circular engraving around the center of the entrance, creating half circles in each of the two doors. Each was divided such that the circle was broken into quarters. On each of the quarters was written one of the four primary Akota traits: wisdom, generosity, bravery, and endurance.

"They'll be waiting in the center room," said Red Moon. "You must go alone from here."

"Thank you, cousin," said Stone, his heart pounding with anticipation.

The cone-shaped building featured a series of cedar platforms lining the circumference. Across from each platform was a series of walkways leading to a cylinder rising up from the center of the conical superstructure. Looking over the railings, he could see the area between the superstructure and the center building was open so that people could look down toward the myriad of plants and small trees on the ground floor. He looked back toward the center of building. Across from him stood another Terillian officer.

"If you will follow me, Magakisca," said the officer, "the Shirt-Wearers are ready for you."

"Lead the way," replied Stone.

Stone and the officer made their way to an elevator platform and began the descent to the ground level.

When the elevator reached the ground floor, Stone looked directly toward the center structure, a tanned animal skin acting as the door.

"This is it," said the officer.

He exhaled forcefully and walked to the entrance. Another deep breath, and he slid the cover to one side and stepped inside.

In the middle of the room was a modest circular table. The center of the table held a small fire, representing the symbolic importance of the council fire. Around the table sat four middle-aged men: the Shirt-Wearer and Senior Fleet Admiral, River, Shirt-Wearer and Marshal, Wolf and the two remaining Shirt-Wearers, Shadow and Falling-sky.

"Magakisca, please join us," said Shirt-Wearer River, motioning for Stone to join them at the table. "I'm sure you are wondering why you have been called here."

"Yes, sir … uh, uncle," replied Stone, sitting.

"I'm assuming you're aware of the problems on Tecela Waniyetu," said River, using the Akota name for Kilo 7.

"Yes," replied Stone. "The Followers of the Word are attempting to take control of the planet. A few weeks ago, a suicide attack killed several members of the planet's ruling council and an Akota ambassador."

"And as a result," added Shirt-Wearer Wolf, "General Nero and one of his brigades were dispatched to provide temporary assistance to the local defense forces."

"I'd heard an Akota brigade had been deployed but didn't know it was Nero," replied Stone.

"These damn Followers are making a mess of everything," interjected Shirt-Wearer Fallingsky. "Ever since that lunatic killed himself, they've spread like a virus across the Dark Zone … taking up so many resources."

"At least the Humani have to deal with them, too," said Stone.

"Perhaps," replied River. "What do you think of the situation, Magakisca?"

"The Saint preyed on the desperation of those in the Echo System, and his martyrdom has allowed his promise of a better afterlife to spread across Dark Zone. But there's no easy solution," answered Stone. "Although their religion, if you can call it that, doesn't promise them anything tangible, so many are willing to follow the ideology because of the desperate living conditions on most Dark Zone worlds. Its fundamental tenants resonate with the hungry, powerless, and oppressed in the Zone. They think their reality is hopeless, so they are willing to die for a chance at a better afterlife."

"Interesting," replied Shirt-Wearer Shadow.

"But what would you do?" asked Shirt-Wearer River.

"Saying it can be solved sets us up for failure," answered Stone. "But there is a chance to mitigate the damage and hopefully, in time, manage it." He looked at each Shirt-Wearer before he continued. "The cats are out of the bag," he added. "And there is no way to catch them all without getting scratched."

"So we do nothing?" inquired River.

"No. We do what we can, but we must understand there is no one hundred percent answer. If that's what you're looking for, you should be prepared for disappointment."

"So, Magakisca," asked Shirt-Wearer River, "what is the ninety percent solution?"

"As soon as you put a percentage on it, we're in trouble. We need to balance a strong physical presence, and force when necessary, with an attempt to show the people of these worlds the life they are currently living can be improved. Show them that death isn't the only path to a better life."

"But their numbers grow so quickly," interjected Shirt-Wearer Wolf.

"We can't just lock down these planets like a prison. First, we don't have the resources, and second, it will only drive more into their fold. I'm sure the Humani are doing this … that's how High Command thinks. So by coming at it differently, we not only drive fewer away with a less oppressive response when possible, but we also represent ourselves as a more tolerant alternative to the Humani."

The room grew silent as the four Shirt-Wearers looked at one another. After a few seconds, Shirt-Wearer River nodded and turned toward Stone. "Magakisca," he said, breaking the silence, "General Nero is dead."

"Dead," replied Stone. "How?"

"Suicide bomber," answered Shirt-Wearer Wolf.

"He was inspecting the site of a recent attack on the inhabitants who supported us and one of the followers was disguised as medic. He detonated a bomb hidden in his gear when Nero and his staff were close enough."

"How many of his staff survived?"

"Just his cousin, Major Vaqa Nero. But he was severely injured."

"That's why we want you to take command," added Shirt-Wearer River. "You are the highest ranking and most experienced Humani soldier."

"And as the majority of Nero's division consists of defectors from Alpha Humana and those he drew support from in the Juliet system ..."

"You want a Humani to lead," interjected Stone.

"We want you to lead," replied Shirt-Wearer Shadow.

A jumbled rush of emotions washed over him. He felt honored to be offered a command by the leaders of the Akota people, but at the same time, their choice only highlighted that, despite his efforts to assimilate, he was still Humani in their minds.

And then there was the assignment. He'd always looked forward to a challenge, but counter-insurgency was a losing game; push too hard and you make enemies out of potential allies, but look soft, and you become easy targets and don't protect those counting on you, which then turns them against you.

"Is this a request or an order?" asked Stone. The Akota military was very different from the Humani.

"Of course it is a request," replied Shirt-Wearer River. "But we must know your choice soon."

"How long —"

"Tomorrow," interrupted Shirt-Wearer Wolf.

"And if I decline?"

"You will stay with Ka-itsenko Ino'ka and her battalion as they plan the attack."

"But you know where you will be of greatest value when the assault on Alpha Humana takes place," added Shirt-Wearer River. "You can be an aid in an attack on Humani ships in orbit … or lead the main force in an attempt to gain control of the Humani government. We just need you to deal with this problem on Kilo 7 first."

He knew the right answer, but he didn't know if it was his answer to give. Mori had tied his future into hers. What would this mean to her

… to them? Then he flashed back to Emily Martin's words to him on *Hydra*.

Don't let these people change you.

"We will eagerly await your decision," said Shirt-Wearer Falling-sky to break the silence.

"I'll do it," replied Stone, almost blurting it as a response to Martin, even though she was systems away.

Chapter 3

"Why have you come to my ship?" asked Admiral Carsis Plaxis.

The silver-haired but still clearly fit Admiral sat confidently at his desk onboard the battlecruiser *Seria Vatri*. Plaxis had a reputation as an excellent officer, and although he never cared for politics, he was as well-known for his loyalty to the Senate and ProConsuls as he was for his tactical skill.

"I am assembling a team to pursue the Traitor once I recover and would like to interview some of your men," replied Martin.

"Well," sighed Plaxis, "I am assuming since you are here in person, your request carries the weight of the ProConsul."

"Not that that matters, but yes."

"I see." Plaxis looked down at his desk and exhaled. "Very well then, Paladin Martin," he continued. "Who do you want to see?"

"I would rather discuss the list in private, Admiral," said Martin with a glance to Plaxis's Chief of Staff, Commodore Chera.

"That is an unusual request," mused Chera.

"Perhaps," retorted Martin. "But it isn't a request," she added with a confident smile.

"But —"

"Please excuse us," said Plaxis to Chera.

Martin could see Chera fume, but he wouldn't challenge Admiral Plaxis, or her. "Aye, Admiral," conceded Chera, casting a cold gaze toward Martin. "I'll be available if you need me."

"He won't," replied Martin.

As Commodore Chera exited Plaxis's in-port cabin, Martin stepped closer to the admiral's desk.

"Here is a list of potentials."

Plaxis leaned forward from his chair and picked up the note.

Martin subconsciously placed her good hand on the grip of her pistol. If Plaxis wasn't the man Nero said he was, it would all be over. She felt her heart pounding in her chest as Plaxis read the note:

I KNOW THE TRUTH ABOUT THE XEN AND THE FIRST FAMILIES. NERO SAYS YOU CAN BE TRUSTED. NEED A SECURE PLACE TO TALK.

Plaxis's glance shot up toward Martin. His eyes were wide but he made no quick movements. Martin gripped her pistol in its holster as the two stared at each other. Slowly, Plaxis rose from his desk, gripping the slip of paper.

"This," said Plaxis as he held the note toward Martin, "is quite the list. What do you plan to accomplish with this?"

Martin leaned forward, placing her hands on the admiral's desk. "Put an end to those that have proven themselves enemies of the Humani people," she said slowly.

Plaxis stood silent. Martin knew Plaxis was also taking a chance by trusting her. From his perspective, it could be a trap to test his loyalty.

"You can speak freely here. This room is out of earshot of the ProConsul."

Martin let out a sigh of relief. "I have to —"

"First, Paladin," interrupted Plaxis. "How do I know this isn't a trap?"

"It isn't, Sir."

"Well, I guess I have no choice. If it is a trap, you'll most likely kill me on the order of the ProConsul. If it isn't and I refuse, you'll kill me anyway." Plaxis sucked in a deep breath and tugged out the wrinkles in his uniform. "But if I am to die, let it be for my people and not that arrogant, power-hungry bitch," he added.

"Good," replied Martin with a smile. "And don't worry … if I ever do kill you, it will be because I want to, not because someone tells me to. I'm done killing for the wrong reasons."

"Comforting," said Plaxis dryly. "So why have you really come?"

"Not only have I seen Nero and Stone, but they … I … am working with the Terillians in hopes of instigating a revolt here on Alpha Humana to coincide with an attack on the Gateway Station." She wouldn't tell him about Dolus. He didn't need to know, at least not yet, and it was safer to make sure no one person knew everything.

"Attack the Gateway Station?" blurted Plaxis. "And Alpha Humana? There's no way that will succeed. Any attack force jumping near the Gateway Station without the codes will —" He paused, stepping out from behind his desk. "You need the encryption codes."

"Yes," replied Martin.

"Then what? There's no coming back from a move like this."

"That's the plan. According to Nero, there are others among the First Families who want free of the Xen and will join us."

"Who is 'us'?" shot back Plaxis. "Nero can't have more than a brigade — five thousand men, and even though I command two battle groups, only a third would follow me, at best. I don't think we can overthrow Astra Varus and hold off the resultant Xen and Doran attacks with maybe one battle group and a few thousand men."

"What about the others?"

"And just who do you think would join in this revolt?" asked Plaxis.

Martin hesitated. Was Plaxis playing her? Was Astra Varus or one of her minions listening to this conversation? If she gave up the names, not only would the revolt not happen, but any chance of a future rebellion might be destroyed. "I don't —"

"You don't trust me," interjected Plaxis. "Don't forget you're the one that came to me."

"Perhaps it's better if we try to keep things compartmentalized."

"The families I know of are mine, of course, Malius, Vanari, Juli, and some of the Vae. The remnants of the Nero family are split, with some trying to regain favor and the others just trying to avoid reduction in status. But they are under too close of a microscope to be involved until the last minute. Then there are the Great Eastern Mountain Families."

Plaxis had named most of the families Nero had mentioned. If Astra knew this information, and she would if Plaxis was loyal, she would have acted already … probably. Martin suddenly yearned for the simplicity of battle. Being a spy was much too complicated. "Screw it," she declared. "Apparently the Centius are dissenters, as well."

"Interesting," replied Plaxis. "And there may be others who are smart enough that no one else knows about them. But even then, that won't be enough."

"I can't discuss the plan in detail, but there will be enough support from the Terillians to take key areas and then defend strongholds until the word can be spread to the population —"

"Terillians on Humani soil?" replied Plaxis anxiously. "And you trust them?"

"I've never trusted a Ter," replied Martin. "But Stone does, and I trust him."

"And if we tell the commoners what we have done — for centuries — they will destroy the First Families. You would become the lapdogs of the Terillians or let our world slip into the chaos of the mob?"

"I will die before I am ruled by a Terillian," growled Martin. "But you know as well as I do that our people aren't truly ruled by a Humani right now. Astra Varus may be the boot, but the Xen hold the keys to our chains."

"You are saying the right words, Paladin," replied Plaxis. "But —"

"Call me Major, sir," interrupted Martin. "Paladin is a title of the ProConsul."

"Very well, Major," continued Plaxis, "I am reluctant to stick my neck out for a plan that I have no idea will succeed."

"It will," said Martin. "It has to. Nero developed it, the Terillian leadership support it, and Stone agreed to it. It's risky ... but it can work."

"And what do you need from me other than the codes?"

"I will return to you in about four months and provide you with more details. Then, when the time comes, bring your fleet near the Gateway Station for a training exercise. Once you're there, send out an electron spin burst with the codes for the next day to a location I will provide the next time we meet. The Terillians will jump and attack Gateway Station. When that happens, join the fight with us."

"You do understand carrying out a revolt onboard a warship, not to mention the entire fleet, will not be easy. I can move a few officers around to stack the deck on a few ships, and once the battle starts, I can come up with a story to get others to continue to fight the ship, but in the end, pretty much every ship is going to have its own little civil war to fight."

"At least if they're fighting each other, they won't be fighting the invasion force," replied Martin.

"Humani killing Humani so that a Terillian task force can attack Alpha Humana," said Plaxis, shaking his head. "If this fails, we'll be crucified." He paused. "And if we succeed …"

"We'll have a whole lot of new problems," replied Martin. "But they'll be our problems, not the Xen's."

"I'm in," declared Plaxis.

***

"So what's the news?" asked Cassandra Orion, shoving a piece of bread in her mouth.

"You assholes blew up my ship," grunted Rickover. "That's the news."

Mori, sitting across from Stone, rolled her eyes.

"It was *my* ship, Rickover," replied Orion, still chewing. "And you're gonna have to let that go."

"Well, the engine room was mine," grumbled Rickover.

Stone looked forward to the occasional breakfasts shared by those he'd been with on *Hydra*. Although he, Mori, Katalya, and Magnus had been training for the boarding of the Humani capital ships and Orion had assumed command of a squadron of Foxtrot fighters, the crew and passengers of the *Hydra* still managed to meet up once a week for breakfast. What he did not look forward to was the first few minutes of each meal when Rickover unfailingly reminded everyone they had destroyed his baby.

"Aren't you busy enough building those gadgets to shut down the Hanmani reactors?" asked Mori.

"That was easy," replied Rickover. "Just a simple matter of inductance. Now the fleet maintenance officer has asked me to join his inspection team."

"There won't be ship in the fleet fit to fly," joked Orion.

"If their systems are in good order —"

"Joking," interrupted Orion. "Anyway, I really was asking about the news," she continued, looking toward Stone. "What's this I hear about you taking over Nero's division?"

Startled, Stone coughed, nearly spitting out his mouthful of eggs.

"What are you talking about?" asked Mori, first looking toward Orion but quickly shifting her gaze to Stone. "What is she talking about?"

Stone felt as if every eye in the massive mess hall turned toward him.

"I … it just happened yesterday," said Stone, knowing the time made no difference.

He glanced slowly toward Orion, who tightened her jaw, curling one side of her mouth. "Sorry," she mouthed.

"So that was your meeting?" acknowledged Mori with a nod, her lips turned tightly inward.

He knew she was surprised … and hurt. But he needed time to prepare himself before he talked to Mori about leaving. "Yes. I —"

"Thanks for …" She paused. "I've got work to do," she added as she rose from the table. "I have an attack to plan."

"But Ino'ka —"

Mori turned from the table without acknowledging Stone and began to walk toward the exit.

"What was that about?" asked Rickover.

"Are you serious?" replied Orion.

"What? Stone's got a new job … one he's qualified for. Everyone's got a new job after you people killed *Hydra*."

"Are you —" Orion stopped. "Never mind." She turned toward Stone. "You better go after her."

"Better not," interjected Katalya.

"I have to," replied Stone, rising from the table.

"Just give her time."

"I don't have time," said Stone.

Stone rushed across the mess hall into the passageway. Turning to his left, he saw Mori leaning against the wall, looking up toward the ceiling.

"Ino'ka," said Stone.

"Damn it," cursed Mori. "Just leave me alone."

"I can't," he replied as he stepped toward her, placing his hand on her shoulder.

"You don't get to decide," she snapped, her eyes wet with tears. "But I guess you're getting good at making decisions about us," she said coldly.

"I didn't mean —"

"Just leave me alone for a few —"

"I'm leaving tomorrow," interrupted Stone. "We need to —"

"Tomorrow?" guffawed Mori as she turned partially away from Stone and took in a deep breath. "Well, *General Stone*, good luck. I'm sure you'll be glad to be with your own people again."

"That's not fair," he replied, turning her shoulders so she was facing him.

"Fair," growled Mori. "Were you even going to tell me or just leave me a note on the pillow?"

"I was going —"

"Hmm," interrupted Mori.

"Damn it, just listen for a minute," he continued, gripping her arms tightly.

"Let go," she demanded, breaking his grip on her arms. "I'm not some helpless Hanmani maiden you can order around."

"I wasn't trying to —" Stone paused. "Damn it, you know this is the right thing for me to do. My place should be on Alpha Humana when the attack —"

"Your place," interrupted Mori, "should be with me."

He didn't know how to make this right, but he also knew he would be much more valuable to both the Akota and the Humani people by leading Nero's division. It was the logical thing — the right thing — to do.

Stone stepped toward Mori and gripped her arms again. She didn't resist but turned her gaze away from him. "I want to be with you," he said softly. "My whole existence has changed because of you. But —"

"You've made your decision, Magakisca," she said calmly, looking up toward Stone and brushing away her tears. "I am sure you'll perform well in your new assignment."

"I don't want an assignment to change how we feel about each other."

Mori let an exasperated laugh escape. "You're not in the Humani military anymore. Everything is connected. Just like a star warms a planet and the winds create the ocean waves, one action impacts the others … how can it not be connected? If you don't think of the Great Circle when you make these decisions, you are thinking only of yourself."

"Myself," snapped Stone, his pulse quickening. "If I'd been thinking about myself, I would have turned down the offer and stayed with you." He took in a deep breath, his frustration mounting. "If I had been thinking of only myself, I would be a fucking Humani general and would have left you in that —" Stone froze, realizing he had gone too far. "I didn't —"

"That's okay," said Mori, her voice cracking as she cut him off. "At least all the trouble I've put you through has paid off in a promotion … General Stone. And in case you missed the salutes while you were stuck with us …" Mori stood stiff as a board and raised her right arm in a salute any Guardsman would have been proud to give. "Congratulations, General Venarius Tyler Lucius Stone," said Mori, ignoring his Akota names. "You can once again be a hero to the proud Humani race." Her normally beautiful fierce green eyes looked dark as she dropped her salute and walked away. "And don't follow me."

Stone stood motionless, wondering if he had lost the first woman he truly loved.

***

Mori exhaled a short, quick breath while standing outside of the canvas door to the wichasa wakhan onboard *Winterfall*. If anyone could help her sort out her feelings, it would be the spiritual advisors. Her heart pounded as she wiped the tears from her face. She had tried for hours to tell herself that Stone was doing what was best for the Akota, but all she had done was fall deeper into a sea of doubt and anger.

The canvas covering slowly opened, and an old man poked his head out. His hair was graying, and he had two thin, white lines running down each side of his cheek from his eyes to his jawline.

"Ino'ka," said the man, "what brings you to us?"

"Uncle," she replied, showing respect for his position. "I need …" She inhaled deeply. "I am lost."

"Enter, Ino'ka," said the man with smile. "Let us talk."

Mori stepped into the room, lit only by the fire at the center of the room.

The floor was covered with animal furs, and the flickering light of the fire illuminated bones dangling from the ceiling.

"Sit, warrior," said the man.

Mori sat next to the fire, the smoke wafting up toward her. The slight burning sensation, punctuated by the smell of sage, began to calm her.

"What troubles you?" asked the old man as he sat across from her.

"I am unbalanced, uncle. I don't know what is right and what is wrong."

"Is this about Magakisca's assignment?"

She leaned back. "How did …" Of course he knew. The Shirt-Wearers would have spoken with him, as well. The advisors were the keepers of everyone's secrets and dreams. She took a breath, hoping the sage would further calm her. "In my head I know why he was chosen and also why he accepted, but …" She closed her eyes, inhaling heavily and looking down toward the furs on the floor. "But in my heart I feel betrayed because he chose to leave … and that he did not consult me."

"So you are conflicted?"

"I feel angry … hurt. And then I feel bad for feeling that way."

"And you want to know what is right?"

"Yes," huffed Mori. "I need to know: How I am supposed to feel?"

"You feel how you feel, warrior."

Sometimes the wise ones could be infuriating. "I'm sorry, uncle. But that isn't very helpful."

The man threw another branch on the fire. "The fire is comforting, is it not?"

"It is."

"What makes it comforting ... other than the sage?" he smiled.

"It warms me."

"But you wouldn't realize the warmth unless you were cold."

"I guess."

"So if it wasn't for the cold, you wouldn't appreciate the warmth and it wouldn't comfort you in the same way."

She began to understand.

"What makes the Great Circle work, brave warrior?"

Mori tilted her head. "Uncle?"

"Why does it work?"

"It remains unbroken? It represents the life cycle?" She knew it represented everything. What did he want to hear? "It represents the seasons?"

"The seasons?" asked the man. "What about them?"

"The cold and darkness of the winter gives way to the sunlight and rebirth of spring and —"

"Wouldn't our ancestors have been better off without the winter?"

Her brow furrowed. "I don't understand."

"When our ancestors roamed the plains on the First Planet, wouldn't they have been better off without the snow and the cold? Without the death of the crops and the scattering of the herds of the buffalo?"

"I never thought about it," replied Mori. "Maybe?"

"That is a very indefinite answer for a warrior. A Ki'etsenko."

"I just don't understand, uncle."

"You think we would be better without the winter."

"Yes," she replied, feigning certainty.

"What did the ancestors do during the winter?"

"The clans broke into family groups and took shelter in the valleys."

"And?"

"The grandfathers told stories to the children and the husbands and wives spent time together because they couldn't during the other seasons between the hunts and warfare."

"And what came from the grandfathers and the husbands and wives?"

"The grandfathers passed on our traditions and wisdom and the husbands' and wives' unions continued our people's existence."

"So is the winter bad or good?"

"I know you are trying to teach me, uncle. I guess it can be both."

"Just like the warmth of the fire needs the contrast of the cold to provide comfort, your separation makes the union stronger when two that have parted are again together. And like the winter, you cannot focus on the negatives of a situation. If you look closely enough, you will see that everything has a place in the Great Circle."

"So I should let him go?"

"He will go. It is not up to you."

"I didn't … I mean, should I let him go in my heart?"

"To know if the spring will be a good one bringing forth growth or if it will bring floods, you must stay in the valley and last out the winter. You can also stamp out the fire for fear that it will burn you, or you can step back into the cold for a short time so that its warmth is new and comforting upon returning to it."

A smile came to Mori's face.

The old man returned the smile.

Mori rose to her feet, a weight lifted from her soul. "Thank you, uncle."

"You are welcome, warrior," he replied.

She turned to exit the room.

"Ino'ka," added the man as he sat by the fire. "You feel relieved that our talk has lessened your burden. And that is good. But like you prepare for the freeze of winter and the bite of fire when it grows out of control, you must look into yourself and ask why letting him go when the cold comes was the question you posed instead of what you need to do to keep him in your heart during all seasons."

Mori turned quickly toward the old man.

He had moved away from the fire and had
curled up on the floor with his back to her,
covering himself in a fur.

He would say no more.

Chapter 4

Stone stood on the tarmac awaiting his newly assigned adjutant. Once he arrived, Stone would board his transport and take command of the effort to stop the spread of the Word on Kilo 7.

But his mind was elsewhere.

After their argument, Stone had given Mori her space. He waited until after dinner before returning to their shared quarters. And then he waited all night for her to return.

But she didn't.

Now, having been awake all night, he stood waiting for a fellow Humani officer but was only able to think about Mori and what he may have lost. Although he faced the platform where his transport was scheduled to land, he periodically glanced toward the exit of the hangar in hopes Mori would be there. After a few minutes, the roar of a transport arriving overhead caused

Stone to look upward. Coming in from the north, the Akota transport came to a hover and then descended toward the landing platform.

Focusing on the door as the transport locked into its mooring, Stone could make out the insignia of a wolf's head with the phrase "Death before Tyranny" written in Humani. After a quick glance toward the hangar, he turned back toward the transport as a figure emerged from the open hatch.

The officer was tall and thin with salt and pepper hair and a well-trimmed beard. As the man brushed off his Terillian confederation uniform, Stone recognized the rank insignia to be that of a Humani colonel. Following the colonel were two captains and four enlisted men. The enlisted men took up positions at the entrance to the transport. *This must be the guy*, he thought to himself as he began to walk toward the transport.

"Attention on deck!" shouted one of the captains, and the party snapped to attention.

"Good morning, General Lucius Stone," said the colonel, giving a crisp salute. "I am Colonel Taris Vae, former Chief of Staff for General Nero."

"Good morning, Colonel," replied Stone, returning his salute. "And the rest of your party?"

"Sir, may I present Captain Velari Scarus and Captain Gius Juli. Captain Scarus is a member of the logistical staff and Captain Juli is the staff's security officer."

"Gentlemen," replied Stone with a nod toward the captains. "And the enlisted men?" he added as he walked toward the guards.

"Uh, yes, Sir," stammered Vae. "These men are part of the security team assigned to you." The colonel paused, glancing toward Captain Juli.

"Sir," continued Juli, "this is Sergeant Charles, Corporal Thara, and Privates Talla and Rezaro."

"How are you doing, Sergeant?" asked Stone.

"Excellent, Sir," replied the sergeant, "I'm just glad to have a Guardsman leading us."

"Charles?" mused Stone. "There was a Corporal Charles from 2nd Regiment … I believe from Captain Keller's company. I also believe that same Corporal Charles killed a painted-face Akota on Sierra 7 several years back."

"A long time ago, Sir," replied Charles with a slight smile that evaporated as the sergeant continued. "But that's when we were fighting the wrong enemy."

"Very true, Sergeant. Very true. Regardless," he added with a smile, "it's good to see another Guardsman."

"Sir," interrupted Colonel Vae. "If you are ready, we can have Privates … uh —"

"Talla and Rezaro," offered Juli.

"Yes, Talla and Rezaro can collect your baggage."

A smile came to Stone's face. How different the Humani were from the Akota; there was no way an Akota warrior would carry baggage for another because of rank alone. Stone raised the small duffel bag in his hand. "This is it," he replied.

"Very well, Sir. Shall we board?"

A quick glance toward the hangar confirmed Mori wasn't there. "Yes," he sighed.

"We are ready when you are, General," said Colonel Vae. "And I might add, Sir, it is a pleasure to serve under your command."

"Thank you, Colonel Vae," replied Stone.

He had to look one more time.

Turning back toward the hangar, he saw Mori.

She was wearing tactical gear and her hair was tied into two tight braids falling over each shoulder. Even from several meters, he could see her green eyes almost glow.

"Just a minute, Colonel," said Stone, already walking toward her.

Mori stood motionless as he moved closer, but her eyes screamed for him to hurry. Reaching for her, he took her hands in his.

"I'm so glad you came. I was afraid I wouldn't get to see you." He squeezed her hands tightly. "I'm so sorry I —"

"Don't be," she interrupted. "You made what you thought was the best decision. That doesn't mean I have to like or understand it. But it is yours to make."

"I don't want to leave you, but —"

"Stop," she said, placing her hand on his cheek. "I spent several hours with the wichasa wakhan last night and then several more at the range. The truth is, I don't know what this means for our future. But I can't stop you from leading … regardless of what happens to us, it's your nature to lead."

Stone was awash in emotions. He was relieved she had come to see him and that she said she understood, but he was also concerned over how she had said it. "I don't want this to be the end of us."

"I don't either, but only time will tell, Magakisca," she said as a tear ran down her check. "But for now, we both have missions to accomplish."

"Yes," he conceded.

He felt her pulling him toward her and he lowered his head for a passionate, long kiss. As he embraced her, she squeezed tightly.

Placing her hands on his cheeks and slowly pulling away from the kiss, she looked up toward him, tears now flowing. His own vision blurred as tears welled in his eyes.

"Be safe, General," she said with a crack in her voice and a weak smile as she wiped his eyes with her sleeve.

"You too, Major," he replied, relieved there was still hope for them.

"You should go," said Mori, looking over his shoulder. "Your lapdogs await."

"Yes," he replied. "I —"

"When you return," said Mori.

He stared into her green eyes, unable to move.

"Go," she said, urging him to move with her eyes.

"I ..."

Mori let out a long exhale, turned, and hurried back into the hangar.

Stone watched until she disappeared behind the heavy metal door of the hangar.

He took a deep breath. "Time to focus," he said aloud and turned to rejoin to his new staff.

***

Major General Stone sat in the troop compartment of the transport as Colonel Vae began his briefing. The compartment had been modified for staff purposes, with displays replacing the starboard-side troop seating, and the port side of the compartment arranged around a desk embedded with data screens.

"Very well, Sir. I can give you the basics now," said Vae. "The Dark Zone Auxiliary Division, known as the DZAD, is comprised of three brigades. First Brigade is called the Humani or Nero's brigade, and is made up of Humani soldiers and other defectors. It was commanded by General Hara Nero, but he was killed in the attack that killed … most of the Nero family senior officers. Colonel Tiri Scarus has taken command. Current strength is approximately forty-two hundred after taking about three hundred fifty casualties on Kilo 7."

"And the other brigades?" asked Stone.

"Second Brigade is a mixture of rescued slaves and farmers from the Juliet System. It is commanded by a former mercenary named Brand Maxa."

"A mercenary?" asked Stone.

"Yes, General," replied Vae. "He is surprisingly good, if a bit rough around the edges."

"And their strength?"

"Thirty-seven hundred. They are on their way to Kilo 7 onboard Admiral Crow's warships."

"Continue."

"Third Brigade is five thousand strong and consists of others recruited from across the Dark Zone. They are relatively green and currently undergoing training on Luta-tunkan. They are under command of the Akota General Joseph Winterbird."

"How far along are they in their training?"

"They are ready to deploy, Sir," answered Vae.

"What about armor and air support?"

"First brigade is best set for armor and gunship support. They are full up with Humani manning requirements. Second brigade has a few main battle tanks and several light tanks in one combined battalion. Third is straight infantry with no heavy armor elements but fully mechanized."

"Send orders to General Winterbird. Have his brigade ready to depart for Kilo 7 in two weeks. Also contact Akota command. Find out how long it will take to have transportation ready for Third Brigade. Once we have the logistics set up, prepare deployment orders."

"Yes, Sir," replied Vae.

"Have General Winterbird leave ahead of his brigade. He should have an idea of the situation before his men arrive." Stone paused. "And I want to speak with all of my commanders face-to-face … we have a lot to do."

***

ProConsul Astra Varus took a deep breath, holding back her frustration. She hated dealing with the Dorans, especially the authoritative and dismissive Lord General Zorlar. To make matters worse, the Doran commander always required her to meet on his flagship, *Kítrinos Potamós*. Looking across the white marble desk at the proud Doran royal, she spoke.

"Lord General Zorlar," she said with a forced smile. "I am simply asking to have one or two of your regiments support General Vlaxi. If you can do this, the Foxtrot System would —"

"Why do you need Doran troops, ProConsul? Why not pull more troops from sector four? Golf, Bravo, and Charlie System are —"

"The Word —" interrupted Astra, but she stopped as two Doran guards stepped forward. In response, two Praetorians moved forward from their position at the far end of the room. "Forgive me," mouthed Astra with a nod of her head. "Please continue."

Zorlar motioned for his guards to stand down. "As I was saying," continued Zorlar, "Golf, Bravo, and Charlie are firmly under your control, but I have seen reports that a large number of troops are still stationed there. Also interesting is the fact that the flow of slaves out of the region is more like a trickle."

"There … there have been complications, Lord General," replied Astra, trying hard to cover her disdain with subservience. "The spread of the Word has complicated matters and driven our casualty rates up drastically."

"I do believe the problem with these religious fanatics is one of your own making, and your casualties are no concern of mine."

Astra's skin grew hot. She was not used to being refused — and even less used to having a mistake thrown in her face. "I …" She paused for another deep breath. "I am handling the problem with the Word fanatics. But I must ensure that we, in the name of the Xen emperor, have complete control of the area. Once that is done, the supply of slaves will flow. After all, we both share the goal of supporting the emperor and bringing glory to the Empire."

Zorlar stared blankly at Astra. She could hear the sound of her breathing during the long, uncomfortable silence.

"And we must bring glory to the Empire," said Zorlar, breaking the silence. "You may have one of my brigades to support your efforts in the Foxtrot system. But they will still answer directly to me and will be an independent command. Your General Vlaxi may call upon them for support, but all operational decisions will remain with General Dal and myself."

"As always, Lord General Zorlar, your leadership and wisdom honors your clan and the Doran Kingdom."

"And your drive to bring glory to the Empire brings honor upon yourself and your people," replied Zorlar flatly. "But ..." Zorlar leaned forward from his chair. "... if this is a ploy to support some separate Humani agenda ..."

"I assure you it is not," replied Astra, lying.

"I will not allow one drop of Doran blood to be spilled for your own personal schemes."

"My only desire is to serve the Emperor."

"We shall see," replied Zorlar, leaning back into his chair. "And now, if we are done?"

"Of course, Lord General Zorlar," replied Astra, rising from her chair and giving the Lord General a slight nod of subservience. "And again, the Humani people are grateful for your wisdom and support in our efforts to support the Empire."

Zorlar returned her nod. "As always, you have proven yourself to be a loyal member of the Empire … and a skilled negotiator."

"You honor me," replied Astra. "Now if I may take my leave?"

"Very well, ProConsul."

Astra turned to exit the room. As she reached the door the two Praetorians pivoted and fell in behind her as she stepped into the hallway. Awaiting her in the passageway were two Humani senators.

"ProConsul," said Senator Marcus Sarius, "I hope your negotiations were successful."

"Of course they were," shot back Astra, walking past Senator Sarius and his companion, Senator Julius Lucretia. "Come with me."

Astra's frustration simmered as she walked through the passageway of the Doran warship. She had been able to get what she wanted, but she despised having to grovel to get it. In a few moments she strode through the door of her transport.

"Get me off this fucking ship," she ordered as the transport doors closed.

"Yes, ProConsul," replied General Vispa, who had been awaiting her return.

"And General Vispa," continued Astra. "In my room ... now."

Astra, with General Vispa and the Senators in tow, stormed into her small but plush stateroom onboard her private transport. She walked next to her desk, picking up a large crystal image of the Humani Eternal Flame statue. As the door slid shut, she released all of her frustration with a grunt as she threw the statue against the wall.

"ProConsul —"

Astra raised her hand to silence Senator Lucretia. She exhaled heavily as she smoothed the sides of her dress, calming herself. "His Excellency ..." She thought she might choke on the words, even if she was mocking him. "His Excellency Lord General Zorlar has authorized a brigade of Doran troops to support our efforts in the Foxtrot System."

"That is good news, ProConsul," replied Vispa.

"General Vispa," continued Astra, "order General Vlaxi to detach his best brigade and have them transferred to General Attia in the Bravo system."

"Yes, ProConsul," acknowledged Vispa. "But I must advise that even with the support of the additional troops, removing a full brigade will delay our success in the system and undoubtedly result in more Humani casualties."

"Thank you, General," said Astra, slowly raising her head toward him. "Now pass the order to General Vlaxi."

"Of course, ProConsul."

"The addition of a full brigade in the Bravo region will definitely help bring the zealots under control," added Senator Lucretia.

"And it will increase both the number of captives which we can send to both Dolus and to the Xen," said Astra. "Will it not, General?" she asked with a glance toward Vispa.

"Yes, ProConsul, it will."

"It had better. I am growing tired of bowing down to these Dorans just to keep our plans on schedule … a schedule which is already behind," she added, looking toward the Senators.

"The numbers are lower than expected, ProConsul," acknowledged Sarius. "But we did not expect Tali Vena to —"

"To lose his mind and start believing his own bullshit?" interrupted Astra. "When the 'Saint' unleashed his zealots — zealots that were supposed to be shipped off to the Xen and to Dolus — on the Dark Zone, he made a mess of our plans." She stepped toward the Senators. "Plans you had guaranteed me would succeed."

"And they will, ProConsul," said Lucretia reassuringly. "There have been delays, but with some minor modifications, such as freeing up more troops as you have so masterfully done, this plan will still work."

"Do not try to flatter me like one of your whores," replied Astra. "Not only does the fate of our people and glory of the First Families depend on this plan … but so do your lives. Ensure that it succeeds."

"It will, ProConsul," replied Sarius.

"It had better," snapped Astra. "And I am tired of trying to guess what the Dorans are up to. Do we have any news from our operatives?"

"We have nothing on Lord General Zorlar," replied Sarius. "As you know, he rarely leaves his flagship."

"And his staff?"

"Most follow his lead but a few make occasional trips to the recreation areas in Mt. Castra, Tacitus Major, and Varus City."

"And what do they do there?"

"What most soldiers do, ProConsul," said Lucretia. "Drink and frequent the recreation houses."

"The Dorans are sleeping with Humani women," said Varus, her stomach turning at the thought.

"Apparently their anatomies are very similar to ours," answered Lucretia. "And from what our sources say, they have a reputation for being rather … ah …"

"What is it?" ordered Astra.

"They will have sex with anything humanoid and take pride in the variety of their conquests," came a voice from the corner of the room.

"I'm glad to see you have joined the conversation," said Astra to a plain-dressed man leaning against the bulkhead.

The man was tall and thin with a bald head and a well-trimmed goatee. A thin smile came to his face. "Of course, ProConsul," replied the man. "You don't pay me to waste your time, so I only talk when I have something valuable to say."

"Well," replied Astra, "what do you have?"

"Most of those that hit the recreation houses are company and field grade officers. They usually come in waves, most likely between their duty cycles. They hit the bars for a few hours and finish up the night at the recreation houses ... usually with two to three girls."

"Disgusting," interjected General Vispa.

"Really," replied Astra with a laugh. She knew Vispa had his own private stable of whores. "Don't hide jealousy by feigning contempt." Content with humiliating the general, she turned back toward the mysterious man. "Continue, Mr. Artemis," said Astra.

"The flag and staff officers occasionally visit the recreation houses and a few have offered to pay to bring the girls back to their ships."

"Have any agreed?" asked Lucretia.

"From what I hear, a few have begged to go, but their house managers have refused. Some have still tried … a few have managed to sneak out with their Doran lovers."

"Really?" replied Astra.

"Apparently the Dorans love the ladies and the ladies love the Dorans," said Artemis with a smile.

"Then that will be the way," said Astra. "Mr. Artemis, contact your Association friends. I want their best female agents in every recreation house in every city the Dorans frequent. I want the most beautiful, manipulative, and heartless agents. Money is not an option."

"As you wish, ProConsul," replied Artemis.

"And I do not want them wasting their time with any Dorans below the rank of Colonel. Their job will be to get an invitation by one of the officers to join them on their ship. And they will say yes."

"But what about the house managers?" asked Sarius.

Astra slowly looked toward the senator. She said nothing but stared at him coldly.

"I will make sure they are compliant," added Artemis.

"Thank you," said Astra, still staring at Sarius. "I doubt the manager of a stable of prostitutes would say no to an agent of the ProConsul, do you, Senator?"

"Of course not, ProConsul," replied Sarius.

"Mr. Artemis," continued Astra, "please go to the communications officer and send the message to the Association Council via electron spin."

"As you wish, ProConsul," replied Artemis, who quickly turned and exited the room.

"Do we have to deal with that trash?" asked Lucretia as the door slid shut behind Artemis. "And, please forgive the question, ProConsul, but why do you call him 'mister'? No one even knows his real name."

"That trash, Senator Lucretia, has offered me information that your agents have not been able to obtain the entire time the Dorans have been in orbit around our planet," retorted Astra, the volume of her voice increasing as she spoke. "And the fact he does not have a name is part of the reason he is effective. The fact he is effective is why I pay him a general's salary. Does that satisfy your curiosity, Senator?"

"Yes, ProConsul. I meant —"

"Excellent," replied Astra, activating her communications panel. "Pilot, get me off this damn ship."

Chapter 5

Martin clinched her jaw and her right arm tensed as the medical tech removed the regrowth chamber from her left hand and Dr. Travarus pressed against the skin of her new appendage. "Damn it," she grumbled.

"It will be a little sensitive at first," said Travarus.

"A little? That's not what I'd call it," replied Martin, wincing. "It feels like it's on fire."

"Everything is new, Paladin. The skin … the nerves. Your hand has to relearn what each sensation is and right now it senses everything as pain."

"Awesome. How long will this last?"

"Usually a few weeks, but the more you use it, the sooner you will regain proper sensation and full function. You will just need to work through the pain."

"The story of my life," mouthed Martin. "When I can start working it?"

"Immediately. As long as you can stand the pain. We will have you attend therapy three times a week until function is restored, but the most important thing is that you just start using it."

"How long until I'm back to one hundred percent?"

"For normal replacement it usually take about four to six months. But you, of course, are getting the best care. You should be in fighting shape in three months."

"I'm in fighting shape now. And I need to be one hundred percent in less than two."

"That will be entirely up to you. But for now, you have another appointment."

"With whom?" she asked. The sound of the medical bay opening drew Martin's attention. She looked up to see a Praetorian standing at the entrance. It was an officer, not the usual enlisted errand boys sent by Astra Varus. "Of course."

"Paladin Martin," boomed the Praetorian officer. "The ProConsul requests your presence."

"Well if it's a request —"

"It is not."

"No shit, Praetorian," shot back Martin. "Do they remove your sense of humor with your brains in the same operation?"

The Praetorian stood motionless at the entrance. "The ProConsul is waiting."

"Well, we can't have that? Can we?"

"No we cannot, Paladin. Now please —"

"I'm coming, you fucking robot," she cursed. "Just let —" She grimaced as her new hand pressed against the arm of her chair to help her stand. She shot a glance toward Dr. Travarus.

"Keep using it," replied the doctor. "And don't keep the ProConsul waiting."

"Thanks. for the advice," said Martin, turning toward the Praetorian. "Alright precious, lead the way," she added, walking past the officer and stopping in the center of the passageway.

"Why must you always be so petulant and tactless?" asked the Praetorian as they began to walk.

"Well, Lieutenant … what is it … Oxia," replied Martin. "My job isn't to talk pretty and kiss First Family asses like yours."

Oxia stopped and turned to face Martin. The tall Praetorian looked down toward the Paladin. Martin returned his gaze.

"Even the most ferocious dog needs to be put down when it forgets who its master is … maybe you should remember that, Paladin Martin. And that's all you are … a loud, brash, undomesticated bitch."

Martin stepped close. "Why Praetorian, are you sweet on me?" she smiled. "Talking pretty words like that make me all gooey inside."

"You're a perfect example of why a commoner should never be given the power you have."

"And you're a perfect example of why every commoner should have as much power as me."

"I cannot wait until the Traitor is killed so you can go back to being … no one. Like the rest of your insignificant family."

Martin's heart pounded but she held back. She couldn't let every First Family asshole get to her or she would never finish her mission. "How 'bout you just take me to the fucking ProConsul?"

"Gladly."

***

"I am glad you could find time in your busy schedule to see me, Paladin Martin," said ProConsul Astra Varus.

"I am sorry for the delay, ProConsul," replied Martin, still holding her salute.

"Very well," huffed Astra. "I do not feel like playing games with you today."

"Yes, ProConsul," said Martin, dropping her salute but remaining at attention. "Why have you summoned me?"

"Your regeneration chamber has been removed, so now it is time to talk about getting back to your mission. Colonel Travarus has told me it will take three to four months."

"I will be ready in six weeks, ProConsul."

"That is aggressively optimistic," replied Astra. "But that is why you were chosen for this task."

"Trust me, ProConsul. You have no idea how much I want to complete my mission."

"Then how is your team progressing, Paladin?"

"I have begun looking but may need to continue adding to the team."

"And whom have you chosen?"

"Most will be from Elite Guard units. I have already picked Lieutenants Marcus Plaxis and Jeremia Messer. Next I will speak to Captain Desro and First Sergeant Shara. I also plan to talk to Gunnery Sergeant Mack from the Marines. I would still like to add a few more —"

"Very good," interrupted Astra. "Then might I suggest one of my Praetorian officers, Lieutenant Oxia?"

Martin glanced over to Oxia, who returned an obnoxious smile. "And by suggest, you mean it is an order."

"It is a recommendation from your ProConsul, Paladin Martin," replied Astra. "Take it as you please."

Martin let out a small sigh, the only hint of her frustration. She couldn't say no to the ProConsul and now she would have to deal with one of her henchmen on her team. He could muck the whole thing up but she didn't have a choice. "Welcome to the team, Praetorian." She turned back toward Astra. "But your little pet will have to understand I am in command and follow my orders."

"My Praetorians are much better at following orders than some of — what did you call them? — my pets. At least they know their place. Don't you, Praetorian?"

"I do, ProConsul," replied Oxia. "And I will follow the Paladin's orders … as long as they do not contradict yours."

"Wonderful," escaped from Martin's lips.

"What was that, Paladin?"

"I am sure Praetorian Oxia will make an excellent addition to the team."

"When do I start?" asked Oxia. "I need to have my baggage —"

"Your bag — whatever. I will have the details sent to you via secure message tomorrow. But, if the ProConsul will excuse me, I have another meeting to attend … that is, if the ProConsul is done with me."

"I am," said Astra. "But do not forget the clock is now ticking."

***

"But we must send a message to those that would follow the Word," demanded General Maxa, slamming his hand against the briefing table.

"Your 'messages' usually end bloody, General," replied General Winterbird. "How is this going to sway the inhabitants to —"

"Sway them," interrupted Maxa, his tall, powerful frame tight with anger. "They either join us or —"

"We kill them?" posed Stone, standing from his chair. He had listened to his generals argue for the last ten minutes and decided it was time to say his piece. "If we kill one hundred in a town of five thousan, what good will that do us?"

"It will let the other forty-nine hundred know they must follow," said Maxa.

"Or drive them into the hands of the Followers of the Word," added Colonel Scarus.

"And are we here to gain control of the planet or keep it safe for the inhabitants?" asked General Winterbird.

"Doing the first will take care of the second," answered Maxa.

"Then the people of Kilo 7 will trade a religious war for the yoke of dictatorship," said Stone.

"Let them have the yoke," replied Maxa. "If it means they stop killing each other."

"We need to get at the Bishops," offered Scarus. "They are the ones behind it all. If we can stop them, it will allow us to stop the spread."

"But over the last month we've seen that every time we kill a Bishop, one of the Priests rises to take his place," said Winterbird. "We need —"

"We need to kill them all!" shouted Maxa. "Just let my brigade loose and —"

"Enough!" ordered Stone. "This is not just a military problem. It is much more complicated." Stone continued, activating the global map on the briefing table. "We can't be seen as another oppressor. They will either follow us out of fear or be driven into the ranks of the Word; neither will bring lasting stability."

"So we just let the Word threaten the villagers and recruit more followers," posed Maxa.

"No, General Maxa. We defend them and show them that under our protection — not rule — they can grow and prosper. Then we will gain something much more powerful than conscripts."

"And what is that, General Stone?" asked Scarus.

"Allies, Colonel. Allies."

"So we offer the olive branch? What if they take it and poke us in the eye?" said Maxa.

"There is no easy answer to this," replied Stone. "If we come across as oppressors, we drive a wedge between us and them. And if we are too soft, our casualties — and those of the inhabitants — will continue to rise."

"So what are your orders, General? The stick or the carrot?" asked Colonel Vae.

"Both. Focusing on the western land masses, we set up perimeters around the major cities to control access to the cities. Within the perimeters, however, we let the indigenous law enforcement and military run the day-to-day business while providing quick response units to assist them if they get in trouble. I also want a tenth of each brigade, on a volunteer basis, to be organized into public assistance units to aid with infrastructure and security development."

"And what if these units are attacked or the locals are overwhelmed?" asked General Winterbird.

"Then they get the stick … but we strike only in response to attacks within the cities and only to stop the immediate threat."

"What will we do outside of the cities?"

"General Winterbird's brigade will be responsible for setting up strongholds and sending out patrols into villages."

"And our mission?" asked General Winterbird.

"Communication, General. We will never be able to control every single village, so we will start with the villages in sectors three, five, and six. Move in, speak with the leaders and ask them to migrate into the cities where we can protect them … and keep them away from the Followers of the Word. It will be a tough pill to swallow, but they must understand they will be on their own and possibly caught in the crossfire if they stay out there."

"Won't that just open the door to infiltration of the cities?" asked Colonel Scarus.

"We will need to screen them the best we can at the perimeter," replied Stone, "but some will get through. There will be attacks and resistance from within the cities, but we have to set the expectations and stay the course. The cities of Inotib, Ezah, Elleb, Nager, and Arerrac will be our base cities and have enough room to hold thousands of emigrants." Stone moved his hands over the cities and then toward the outlying areas. "We limit the Word's access to the cities and starve them of recruits from the countryside. From there, Colonel Scarus and 1st Brigade will go after concentrations of Follower units."

"And where does that leave my brigade?" huffed Maxa.

"Your brigade will be responsible for establishing the perimeters around the five cities."

"So Scarus and Winterbird get to seek out and engage the enemy and I get to babysit a bunch of sheep."

Stone's pulse quickened. He already had doubts about Maxa, and this meeting was doing nothing to improve his opinion of the former warlord. "Colonel Scarus is assigned the primary combat role because his unit is the most experienced and the best equipped. General Winterbird is given the engagement role as it is primarily made of up Dark Zone recruits that might relate to the inhabitants."

"So my unit is not capable of —"

"General Maxa!" shouted Stone. He paused, taking in a deep breath. "You were chosen because I know your men will put a stubborn defense against any attacks on your lines." He stepped toward Maxa. "I am not sure how General Nero led this division, but let me make it clear how I do." He locked his gaze on Maxa. "I do expect my officers to ask questions and propose better options; what I do not expect, nor will I tolerate, is insubordination or any displays of brutality toward the civilian population."

"But you're giving the glory to everyone else while my men are relegated to guard duty."

"Your men are providing much needed security for an entire population of future allies, General. And no job is more difficult than that of the sheepdog when the wolves are about. So if you or your men are not up to the task …"

"We will do our duty, General," said Maxa through his teeth.

"Good, General," replied Stone. "And now that we have settled that, Colonel Vae will discuss the details."

"Yes, Sir," said Vae. "I will conduct a brief with all of your field grade officers in four hours. Between our resources and those of the fleet, we are well set to control operations in the western sectors, with one exception."

"And what is that?" asked Winterbird.

"Special operations," replied Vae. "But a battalion of Scout Rangers have been requested and should be arriving within the week."

"More warriors to take the glory," complained Maxa.

Stone slammed the palm of his hand against the table. "If it's glory you're searching for, General, you've come to the wrong place," said Stone. "I have no —"

"They said you were a warrior," interrupted Maxa. "So far I have only seen an administrator. If you are not willing to fight —"

Stone stepped forward, grabbing Maxa's tunic. In one powerful motion, he slammed the warlord onto the briefing table. "You may not want to see the warrior, General," warned Stone. "If you are not willing to follow my commands, you had better resign your commission now, because this is the last time we will have this discussion." Still holding Maxa against the table, Stone drew his sword. "Is that clear, General?"

"Yes, Sir," grunted Maxa.

"Good," replied Stone, releasing his grip. "Now wait outside my office; we have more to talk about."

Maxa pushed himself up from the table and pulled at the bottom of his tunic to straighten it. "As you wish, General," he said with a salute before turning and marching out of the room.

"Definitely not a Humani officer," said Scarus.

"But he and his men are ferocious in a fight," added Vae.

Stone shook his head. "We need more than brute force to win here. And even then it won't look like any victory you have seen before. If we can prevent the Word from taking this planet and leave with the local government able to resist them, it will be a victory … we will never fully defeat the Followers of the Word through combat. It has to be done by the people of this planet … and all the others."

"Yes, Sir," replied the officers in unison.

"Thank you, gentlemen," replied Stone. "Now I must ask you to return to your units while I discuss staff and logistical issues with Colonel Vae."

Again the officers replied and slowly filtered out of the room.

"What is it that you need, General?" asked Colonel Vae as the last of the others left.

"How do you think General Maxa will respond to what just happened?"

"He knows not to challenge you openly again, Sir … but he will work against you whenever he can."

"Will his men follow another commander?"

"Most will, if only for the money. But a few are loyal to him."

"That is a price we may have to pay, Colonel," replied Stone. "Who are suitable replacements?"

"Colonel Waverly is one of Maxa's regimental commanders and seems to be the most level-headed of the group. There is also Colonel Centius. I must admit, I know little of General Winterbird's regimental commanders."

"And what about you, Colonel?"

"I serve as you wish, General."

"Bring the general back in, Colonel."

"He is not going to take this very well, Sir," warned Vae.

"I don't care how he takes it, Colonel. I will not have a man like that under my command."

"Yes, Sir," replied Vae.

Colonel Vae walked over the door, opening it slowly and leaning outside. "General Maxa!" he shouted, "General Stone will see you now."

Maxa strode back into the room, his face still red with embarrassment and anger. "General Stone, I must protest the —"

"General Maxa, as of now you are removed from command of 2nd Brigade."

"You can't do that!" shouted Maxa. "Under what authority?"

"My own authority, General," replied Stone. "You will transfer command to Colonel Vae and you and your staff will depart to Admiral Valley's command ship tomorrow. Any officers feeling they can't serve under anyone other than you will be allowed to join you. In two days, you will depart the fleet and return to Akota territory for reassignment."

"You arrogant son of a bitch," spat Maxa. "Akota territory? What the hell am I going to do with the Ters? I raised this brigade. They are my men and I will command them."

"No, General," replied Stone. "They are mine now."

"Fuck you, Humani," cursed Maxa, stepping close to Stone. "This is just another plot to place more of your robots in command. You and your damn toy soldiers can —"

"You are being replaced because I need someone who can follow commands and is interested in more than killing and plundering."

"I'm thinking only one person needs killin' right now," grumbled Maxa.

Stone saw Maxa reach for his sidearm.

Maxa's pistol had just cleared its holster when Stone grabbed Maxa's wrist, wrenching it backwards and slamming his other fist into the warlord's throat. Maxa's hand contracted, firing a round into the wall as Stone slid his leg behind Maxa's and drove him onto the ground. The warlord let out a groan as his back impacted the floor.

Keeping his grip on Maxa's wrist, Stone grabbed the pistol with his other hand and threw it across the room as he drove his boot into Maxa's chest. With his foot planted on Maxa's chest, Stone drew his sword and swung it downward toward his opponent's neck, stopping just as the blade was about to slice into Maxa's skin.

"Now you see the warrior, you power-hungry bastard," growled Stone. "I was going to just let you disappear, but now you will die."

Stone raised his sword.

Two guards suddenly burst into the room, responding to the gunshot.

"Stand down!" shouted Colonel Vae to the guards.

"Do it!" grunted Maxa, challenging Stone.

Stone gripped the handle of his sword tightly, tightening his body for the downward thrust. But his paused. "No," he said, stepping away from Maxa but keeping his sword leveled at the warlord. "Guards, take the General into custody for assault against a superior officer."

The guards moved forward, restraining Maxa.

"Keep him in the divisional stockade," ordered Vae. "I will call for a courts-martial tomorrow."

"There will be no time, nor enough flag officers," replied Stone. "Transfer him to Valley's flagship tomorrow. Once he's there, General Winterbird can join Admirals Valley and Crow for the hearing. I don't want the Admirals to have to come down here to deal with our trash."

"Trash," laughed Maxa. "You Humani and Ters are all the same. You both claim to be honorable and only concerned with doing your duty, but you're no better than the worst Dark Zone tyrant."

"Take him away," ordered Stone.

"You better kill me, Stone," said Maxa. "Because I promise I will make you pay for this."

Stone waived his hand to the guards and they began to drag Maxa out of the room.

"You'll pay! I swear it!" shouted Maxa as he was pulled from the room.

"You should have killed him, Sir," said Vae.

"That's the difference between an officer and a barbarian, Colonel," replied Stone, sheathing his sword. "I will let him face military justice."

"Yes, Sir," replied Vae.

"But if I see him again, he'll face my blade."

"I fear that you will see him again, Sir."

"Maybe so, Colonel. But tonight, it has been a long day and we should all get some sleep."

***

"General … General."

Stone awoke to Colonel Vae shaking his shoulder.

"W-What is it, Colonel?"

"Maxa. He has escaped."

"What happened? How?" asked Stone, rising from his bed.

"Some of his senior officers must have gotten word he had been detained. A group of twenty or so attacked the Divisional stockade and took him."

"Any casualties?" Stone began to wonder if he should have taken Maxa's life.

"Three guards were injured and one killed," replied Vae.

"Damn it," cursed Stone. "Alert all commanders and fleet captains. We'll need to be prepared for revolts from within his brigade."

"He's already gone, Sir. Admiral Crow reported one of his ships picking up a neutrino burst not associated with any authorized jumps at the same time of the escape. I have sent 3rd Battalion from 1st Brigade to the 2nd Brigade's headquarters, but there have been no further disturbances."

"So the hardcore followers left with Maxa," posited Stone. "Keep 1-3 there until you are confident the unit will be stable."

"Yes, Sir," replied Vae.

"And what about Maxa? What do you think he will do next?"

"He could be anywhere," said Vae, his brow furrowed. "He's probably headed for some remote planet where he can start to rebuild an army and plan his revenge against you."

"Pass a message via electron spin to Akota command and the Shirt-Wearers, but I doubt he will return to Akota territory." Stone let out a heavy breath. "So odds are I'll see him again," conceded Stone. "Just one more person that wants me dead."

"That is a very long list, General," replied Vae with a small laugh.

"And growing, Colonel," said Stone, returning the laugh to hide his concern.

Chapter 6

Martin scanned the smoke-filled officer's lounge. As the rumble of conversations and laughter blanketed the room, she looked for an old friend. A smile came to her face as she saw a lone officer sitting at the far corner of the bar.

"Good to see you, Captain Desro," said Martin, slapping the man on the back.

Desro looked up toward Martin. Her smiled faded when she saw the stern look on Desro's face.

"Good evening … what do I call you, Emily … Major … Paladin?"

"You can call me whatever you like, Venny," she said cautiously.

"I'm guessing you wanted to meet to talk about me joining your team."

"Yes, but —"

"I already helped you capture him once … and I didn't feel right about it then, so —"

"Just shut up, Captain," interrupted Martin. "There's more to it than that, but I don't want to talk about it here."

"Then where?" asked Desro, turning to face Martin.

"Just follow me … please."

"Please," laughed Desro. "That's not a word I think I've ever heard you say."

"Then you know it must be important … just come with me."

"Fine," huffed Desro, tossing a credit chip onto the bar. "But I'm not going after Stone again."

"Then just hear me out for old times' sake."

"I guess you've earned that at least," conceded Desro. "Let's go."

Martin and Desro exited the officer's club and began to make their way across the base. In a few moments they stopped a large building.

"Where are we going?" asked Desro as the two stepped into an elevator.

"My quarters."

Desro pressed the hold button. "Why do we need to go to your quarters?"

"What about earning this one?" asked Martin.

"I'm willing to listen, even though you know my answer is no, but this doesn't make sense. What can't we discuss this at the battalion or —"

"Like I said, it's complicated," replied Martin. "And we needed to find a secure place where everyone could meet," she added, reaching past Desro and pressing the button for her floor.

"Everyone?"

"Well, it's still a pretty exclusive club," answered Martin. "But once we get —"

The elevator door slid open and an Elite Guard First Sergeant snapped to attention.

"Sergeant Shara," said Martin. "Glad you could make it."

"Well, Ma'am, it was an order … wasn't it?"

"Just follow me," replied Martin, "and I'll explain all of it."

Martin, with Desro and Shara in tow, walked the short distance to her quarters. "Come in," she said, activating the door.

"What the hell is all of this —"

Martin raised her hand to silence Desro. "Just a minute … I need to tidy up a bit." As she spoke, Martin pulled an electronic device from her pocket and slowly walked around the room, while Shara and Desro started at each other blankly. "Good. All set," concluded Martin, having checked the room for hearing devices. "Now we can talk."

"Have you lost your mind, Emily?" asked Desro. "What is all this about?"

"No, I just need to make sure your ears were the only ones hearing what I am about to say."

"Damn, Ma'am," said Shara, looking around Martin's room. "Is this your quarters or a museum? You do realize nobody inspects officer's quarters, right?"

"I like it this way," huffed Martin. "And besides, that's not why you're here." She paused, a wave of doubt passing over her. If she was wrong about either of them, it would be the end of the mission, and maybe her life.

"So what is it, Emily?" asked Desro.

Martin sucked in a deep breath and exhaled heavily. "I'm not going to kill Stone. I'm working with him."

"What?" gasped Desro. "But Port Royal …" He paused. "The escape … it was staged."

"Why?" asked Shara, allowing himself to fall into a chair at a nearby desk. "Why would you —"

"Stone's no traitor … he's … when I was hunting him, I found out …" She took another breath. It was time to put all the cards on the table. "I found out that it's all a lie."

"All of what? What are you talking about?" asked Desro. "You're not making any sense."

"Our entire history … it's a lie. The Xen, they were never our allies. They conquered our people generations ago and rewrote our history. They instigated the First Terillian War. And they did it again with the help of the First Families."

"I know you hate the First Families," replied Desro, "but this —"

"It's true!" shouted Martin. "Stone found out and then joined the Akota because —"

"Akota?" asked Shara.

"The Terillians, damn it. He joined the Terillians because he found out the First Families have been working with the Xen to keep our people in the dark … and fighting the Xen's wars for them."

"You can't be serious?" said Desro. "You can't be —"

"Damn it, Venny," interrupted Martin. "Do you really think Stone is a traitor?"

"No. That's why I didn't want to go on another mission. But this …"

"If you believe him … and me then I — we — need your help."

"I do. But help? What help are you talking about?"

Martin's heart pounded. "I need to know you trust me."

"I said I did," replied Desro.

"Sergeant?" asked Martin, turning toward Shara.

"You earned my trust a long time ago on that frozen piece-of-shit planet."

"We need to meet with Stone in a few weeks to confirm the final plans, which will include an assault on the Gateway Station, a secret base Astra Varus has built on Dolus … and an invasion of Alpha Humana to overthrow the First Families."

Desro stepped back. "You're going to help the Ters invade our planet?"

"Venny ... wait," pleaded Martin. "You have to believe me ... the Ters — Terillians don't want our planet ... they're helping us regain it from the First Families. It was Nero's plan."

"Nero!" huffed Desro. "Are you trying to get us sent to Capro Prison?"

"I'm trying to free our people from a prison they don't even know they're in," replied Martin. "A few First Families will support the revolt. It's a lot to take in. I know —"

"A lot to take in," laughed Desro. "And who are these First Families?"

"No one can know everything," replied Martin. "It's better if it stays compartmentalized."

"So you call us here for some kind of cloak-and-dagger meeting and then ask us to join in a revolution ... because you said so."

"Pretty much," replied Martin.

Shara rose from the chair, one hand on his belt and the other resting on his sidearm.

Martin felt her chest beating and felt her breathing increase. Had she made a mistake?

She looked toward Desro, his gaze locked onto her. "If you're gonna —"

"Fuck it. I'm in," said Shara. "If you and Stone are in, I'm in."

"Why not?" said Desro with an exasperated laugh. "I've got no love for the First Families." He paused. "But you better be right."

"I am."

"Then what do we do?" asked Shara.

"We'll start preparations for going after Stone again over the next few weeks while my hand gets back to normal. I also need to pick a few more for the teams to keep suspicions down. One of them should be another Guardsman that we can trust."

"Sergeant Graves," replied Shara. "She doesn't give a shit about the First Families and is a good warrior."

Martin had heard of Sergeant Graves. She was the third female to earn entrance into the Elite Guard after Martin and now-First Sergeant Anna Banks. Her reputation was solid. "How will she react to the truth?" asked Martin.

"I think we'll need to ease her into it, but she's my friend and knows your reputation in the Guard."

"Then have her assigned to the team as well."

Desro stepped close to Martin, gripping her arm.

"If you are wrong, or if this fails …" he said firmly.

"I'm right," she replied. "And it won't fail. It can't. This could mean everything for our planet." She paused, emotion flowing through her body. "And I am honored that you will be by my side."

"For the Republic," declared Shara. "And this time I mean it."

"For the Republic," replied Martin, with a smile. "Now you guys get out of here. I've got more work to do."

***

"Move your ass, recruit!" shouted Master Gunnery Sergeant Stephen Mack. "That obstacle isn't going to climb itself!"

Martin let out a small chuckle as she watched the Marine Drill Instructor run a platoon through the obstacle course. It was that same voice she had heard so many years ago when Staff Sergeant Mack ran Cadet Martin through her first combat course. She watched as Mack trained his recruits but she already knew he was the right man. Not only had he provided the best combat course training she had received from anyone other than Jackson, but his own combat record was impressive. Offered the opportunity to try out for both the Elite Guard and the Praetorians, he turned it down "because he was a Marine," just like he refused three offers for a commission. He was a no-nonsense, in-your-face, ground-pounding grunt ... and most importantly, he had absolutely no desire other than to do what was right by his people.

She watched as the last recruit reached the bottom of "Republic Hill" — the forty-five-degree, one thousand meter hill at the end of the course. Breathing heavily, the young recruit was obviously laboring with his weapon and gear. He slowed, staggering at the base of the hill.

"Are you waiting for a fucking invitation to attack that obstacle, recruit?" shouted the sergeant behind him.

The recruit, clearly exhausted, took another step and stumbled, falling to one knee.

"If you aren't going to attack this obstacle then get off my fucking course and out of my Corps," shouted the sergeant, his face centimeters from the recruit's.

As Martin watched, Master Gunnery Sergeant Mack walked toward the recruit and the sergeant. "Sergeant Patterson, at ease," said Mack.

The sergeant stepped away from the recruit as Mack placed his hand on the young man's shoulder.

"Recruit," said Mack. "Do you want to be a Marine?"

"Yes, Master Gunnery Sergeant," panted the exhausted recruit.

"Well, recruit … Marines rest at the top of the mountain, not the bottom."

"Yes, Master Gunnery Sergeant," replied the recruit before he turned and began trudging his way up the hill.

"Don't say another word to him on the way up, Sergeant," said Mack. "If he makes it on his own, then we know he won't quit."

"Yes, Master Guns," replied the sergeant.

"Are the Marines giving hugs instead of ass-whippins nowadays?" said Martin, walking toward the two Marines.

"Attention!" shouted Mack as he and the sergeant snapped to attention and saluted.

"At ease," replied Martin, returning the salute.

"It's the new Marine Corps, don't you know, Paladin Martin," replied Mack. "They can't all be natural-born killers like a certain cadet I once knew."

"Good to see you Master Guns," replied Martin.

"And you too, Ma'am," answered Mack. "But what brings a Paladin down to see the best warriors in the galaxy … except of course for the Guard, Ma'am?" asked Mack with a smile.

"Of course," answered Martin. "And that's why I'm here. I need you on my team, Master Guns."

"You're going after Stone again?"

"Yes."

"Permission to speak freely?" asked Mack.

"Like you need permission … go ahead."

"That whole traitor thing never set right with me. He isn't the kind to betray his people. Don't get me wrong, I'll follow orders just like any good Marine, but if you know anything —"

"There is a lot I have to tell you Master Guns," replied Martin. "But that's for later. I just need to know if you're in."

"Fuck yeah, I'm in, Ma'am. Can't let the Guard have all the fun."

"Welcom aboard, Master Guns."

Chapter 7

Martin looked down at the watch on her new hand.

"Late," she huffed, looking back toward the busy flow of people on the street below. Standing on the edge of raised platform created for First Family members and high ranking officers, she watched hundreds of people scurry and push themselves along the rolling wave of humanity that made up the lower level streets of Mt. Castra. A small laugh escaped her mouth. Most civilians had no concept of time and promptness, and her cousin, Aria, was no exception. In fact, most interactions with civilians left her either confused, frustrated, or both. She'd almost turned down the invitation for lunch with Aria, but family was family.

Peering through the crowed mass of pedestrians, Martin saw her cousin. Aria weaved around an old man, trying not to make contact with him. She looked up and their eyes met.

"Emily!" she shouted as she forced her way through the pack to Martin.

"Aria," replied Martin, pulling her cousin onto the platform. "I was beginning to think you weren't going to make it."

"What do you mean?" asked Aria. "It's only five after."

"Early is on time and on time is late," replied Martin, only half joking.

"What?"

"Never mind," she laughed. "So where are we eating?"

"Oh!" snapped Aria, unable to control her excitement. "I got us a table at Primum."

"What's that?"

"One of the hottest new clubs in Mt. Castra. It wasn't easy, but my director knows a Senator and —"

"Do they have steak?" interrupted Martin.

"Uh … I'm sure they do, Emily." Aria paused, staring at Martin. "Why did you wear your uniform?" she continued.

"Why wouldn't I?" replied Martin. "What else would I wear?"

"Maybe something that shows off your form a little?"

Martin knew the world her cousin lived in and how important looks were to her success. Aria was one of the best-known dancers in Mt.

Castra. She was as much of a natural at dance as Martin was at combat and in her own way had done well for a commoner — well enough to rub elbows with lower-level First Family members and beautiful enough to get the attention of everyone.

"My form," said Martin, shaking her head, "doesn't have anything to do with us having lunch … or my job."

"Oh, never mind," said Aria with a deep sigh. "Guess you're just … well … you."

"What is that supposed to mean?"

"It's just … how are you ever going find another husband —"

"A husband?" laughed Martin. "Seriously. A husband and moving up the Humani social ladder are the least of my worries."

"Everyone needs to improve the status of their family, Emily. And now that you have been given this high rank, you —"

"That rank comes with a mission I have yet to complete, cousin Aria. And that is my priority."

"I was just saying …"

"I know what you were saying. Can we just have dinner without talking about our family status? I'm starving."

"Sure," huffed Aria. "It's just around the corner."

Aria stepped back toward the edge of the platform, waiting for a window to reenter the mass of humanity.

Martin placed her hand on her cousin's shoulder. "We're not going back down there," she said.

"But I'm a common —"

"And I am a Paladin," interrupted Martin. "We stay up here."

Martin and her cousin leisurely made their way across the platform. After a few hundred meters, Martin felt a tug on her arm.

"It's right over here, Emily," said Aria, pointing down a cobblestone path lined with well-trimmed bushes. "This club is the talk of all the Mt. Castra First Families."

"Fantastic," replied Martin, her opinion of the place plummeting.

"There," said Aria, almost panting with excitement. "See that beautiful classical architecture?"

Martin looked toward the two-story structure. Terra Cotta-tiled angled roofs were supported by massive white pillars surrounding the open-air restaurant. From the entrance there extended a long line of people waiting to enter.

"Nice," said Aria, stopping at the back of the long line. "It's not too bad today."

From their place in line, Martin peered her head outward, looking down the long, winding row of patrons. It was at least twenty-five meters long. "This is a short line?" she asked, reminded of the lines the enlisted stood in on the battlecruisers and orbital destroyers.

"Yeah," replied Aria with an anxious smile. "It usually runs down toward the end of those shrubs. Or at least it has every time I have walked by."

"This is stupid."

"What do you mean?"

"What time is your reservation?" asked Martin.

"Well … now, but everyone has to wait —"

"Come on," said Martin, grabbing her cousin's wrist.

"What are you doing?" asked Aria as Martin pulled her out of the line.

"I'm gonna eat," she replied.

"We can't —"

"Watch me," replied Martin as she — with Aria in tow — walked past the line toward the entrance of the club. As she moved down the line, she noticed at least four colonels and an admiral in the line.

Martin stopped next to a small marble podium, giving a forced smile to an Intelligence Corps colonel. The colonel, next in line, was accompanied by a beautiful blonde woman young enough to be his daughter.

"May I help you?" asked the hostess, her silky raven hair done in a combination of a tight bun and loose braids falling to her shoulders.

Another tug at her shoulder turned Martin's attention to Aria. "We can't —"

"Shh," interrupted Martin, placing her finger to her lips.

"We have an appointment for now," stated Martin. "We would like our seat."

The hostess, her eyes wide, nervously glanced toward the colonel and then returned a blank, anxious stare.

"Emily," said Aria. "We can't just —"

"It's no problem," said Martin, staring into the hostess's eyes.

The hostess looked toward the ground. "I … the colone l—"

"I'm sure the colonel won't mind letting a Paladin be seated before him," interjected Martin. "Now would he?" she added, shifting her gaze toward the colonel.

"Of course not," grumbled the tight-faced colonel.

"Why do we have to wait for this woman?" huffed the girl on the colonel's arm.

"Quiet," fumbled the colonel, his face red with embarrassment. "She's …"

"Because," replied Martin, stepping toward the girl. "This woman answers only to the ProConsul."

"Yes. Yes. Of course," stammered the hostess. "I only see an Aria Martin and guest on the reservation. It did not reflect … I'm sorry,

Paladin … of course, we will seat you immediately."

"Excellent," replied Martin, smiling and giving a wink to Aria. "Immediately sounds nice."

"Yes. Just let me …" The hostess froze, the anxiousness returning to her face. "There … I …"

"What is it?" asked Martin.

"It appears that Regional Magistrate Varus requested a last-minute table, and since the reservation was under the common name Martin and he is the cousin of the Pro —"

"Sequentis Varus?" asked Martin, her skin beginning to boil.

"Yes, Paladin, Magistrate Sequentis Varus."

"It's okay, Emily," pleaded Aria, her face flush.

"Fucking Sequentis Varus!" blurted Martin as the repressed rage of Varus's treason on Golf 2 so many years ago exploded into the present. "There is no way I am giving up my seat to that traitorous coward."

"Emily!" gasped Aria. "You can't say —"

"Where is he?" demanded Martin.

"I don't know —"

"Where!"

The hostess jumped, startled by Martin's explosion. Raising a trembling hand, she spoke. "Over there … table seven."

"Thanks," answered Martin as she turned and strode toward the man Stone had stopped her from killing years ago.

"What are you doing?" begged Aria, trying to keep up with Martin. "Why are you making such a scene? It's just a table."

"It's our table and I'm just getting it for us," answered Martin flatly.

Martin turned the corner as she passed the roaring laughter of the bar. Directly ahead of her was Magistrate Sequentis Varus. Although older and fatter, Martin instantly recognized the coward she knew caused the death of too many of her men on Golf 2. He had a wide, privileged grin painted on his face, a beautiful blonde woman hanging on his shoulder, and sat across from a well-dressed couple. Behind the table stood a sour-looking man with a sidearm attached to his military-style clothing. No doubt he was Varus's personal bodyguard.

With each step, her mind went further back to that day when Varus was under her blade.

Only a few meters away, Martin saw Varus look up from his revelry. His vain smile instantly turned to a scowl. "What are you doing here?" he demanded.

"You're sitting at my table," answered Martin, coldly.

"Your table?" replied Varus with a laugh, although Martin could see tiny beads of sweat begin to form on his forehead. "This establishment is for First Families and their guests, Major, not for commoners."

Martin's skin grew hot. "That's Paladin."

"No matter," he replied. "It's not for my cousin's hunting dog either."

Martin locked her eyes onto Varus's, wanting him to remember just how much she hated him.

Varus swallowed hard, his discomfort beginning to show. "You should move along, Paladin Martin, and let us return to our meal," he said calmly, but Martin saw his hands clinched in tight fists.

"You're in my seat," she replied, her gaze locked on Varus.

"Emily, what are you —"

"Shut up, Aria," interrupted Martin, her hand now resting on her sword. She turned back toward Varus. "You are in my fucking seat," she said mechanically.

"You can't talk to me like that!" shouted Varus with a glance toward the security guard.

The guard stepped forward and Martin responded likewise, gripping her sword. "You stay right where you are or I'll make sure you're carried out of this place," warned Martin.

The guard paused. He glanced toward Varus, his clinched jaw betraying his apprehension.

"Do something!" ordered Varus.

"Yeah," added Martin, tapping her fingers on the handle of her sword. "Do something."

The guard stood motionless.

"This is what I pay you for!" shouted Varus, his voice cracking.

Martin turned toward Varus and smiled. "That's the difference between fighting for money and fighting for a cause; your hired gun isn't going to die for you."

She placed her hands on the table and leaning down toward Varus. "Either you get up from this fucking table or make sure we have another one in the next thirty seconds or I will cause you more pain than you have ever felt in your miserable, privileged life," she whispered before standing erect. "And no one in here can stop me," she added.

Varus stared up at Martin from his chair. That was as close as she could get to giving this asshole a way out. Martin knew she would never get away with killing a magistrate, especially a Varus, regardless of how much she wanted to bleed him out on the floor of the shrine to First Family excess and privilege where he sat. But she was betting Varus thought she just might kill him anyway.

After a long pause, Varus spoke.

"Waiter!" yelled Varus.

Almost instantly a thin, young waiter rushed to the magistrate's table.

"Yes, Magistrate," said the waiter, giving him an accommodating smile.

"Please tell Mr. Finny that Paladin Martin needs a table immediately," said Varus. "And tell him no excuses," he added sternly.

"Yes, Magistrate," replied the waiter with a nod before he scurrying away.

"Wait!" shouted Varus, stopping the waiter in his tracks. "And tell Mr. Finny the table will be on the other side of the club."

Varus glanced toward Martin. She could see the hatred radiating from him. She'd let her emotions almost push her too far, and in the process most likely rekindled a long-dead rivalry with Magistrate Varus. But she couldn't just walk away; that wasn't her style. Even knowing it would be the end of her, and of the plan to save her people from the Xen and the First Families, it still took everything she had not to gut him where he sat.

"Thank you, Magistrate," said Martin, pasting a sarcastic smile on her face.

"Of course. You should follow the waiter and find your table."

"I'll have to thank you personally next time we meet," replied Martin. "And I'll thank your guard too," she added with a glance and a smile toward the guard.

"I'm sure our next meeting will be … very exciting," said Varus, "but for now, you should go."

Martin stood motionless, starting at Varus.

"Now," added Varus.

"Until then, Magistrate," said Martin, breaking the silence.

As Martin turned to walk away, she was met by a short, round, bald man in an expensive suit. "I am Mr. Finny, the manager of Primum," he said, his voice cracking. "Paladin Martin, so very sorry for the confusion. Please allow me to show you to your table."

"Sure," replied Martin.

The manager led Martin and Aria to a small table at the opposite end of the club, as Varus had requested. At the table, the manager pulled out a chair for Aria.

"Ms. Martin," said the manager.

Next, he reached for Martin's chair.

"I got it," said Martin, taking the chair and positioning it so she could see anyone approaching the table. "Thanks."

"Yes. Of course," said Mr. Finny. "Please let me tell you about our specials. We have a —"

"Do you have steaks?" interrupted Martin.

"Uhm … yes, of course. We have the best cuts from several different species and —"

"How 'bout you give me your biggest cut of the meanest animal you have hanging back there, burn the outside, and bring it on out," interrupted Martin. "I'm fucking starving."

"Uhm ..." stammered Mr. Finny. "I ... yes, Paladin ... and you?" he asked, turning toward Aria.

Aria shot a frustrated glance toward Martin. "I would like a salad—dry with ... what accents do you have?"

"We have shali berries, waterfowl sprouts, and seeds from the dragonflower tree."

"They all sound so good," said Aria with a smile. "I'll take all three."

"Of course, ma'am," replied Mr. Finny, "I will get your orders in immediately."

"You eat like a rabbit," joked Martin as Mr. Finny shuffled away from the table.

"No," snapped Aria, "I just don't eat like a highlands bear. And why did you have to make such a scene before? You almost attacked a First Family member — again. I would have thought what happened when we were young —"

"That little prick had it coming, and ... fuck the Varus family," replied Martin, leaning toward Aria. "They're nothing more than vultures living off the slowly dying carcass of the Humani people."

"I had hoped you had outgrown your animosity toward the First Families. And to say what you said to Magistrate Varus, he is —"

"I know exactly who he is," snarled Martin through her teeth. "If he is what you call the best of our society, then we should be wiped from the face of this planet."

"You can't say —"

"I can say whatever I want, cousin. And that traitor to our people caused the deaths of good men."

"I can't believe a Varus would —"

Martin interrupted with a laugh that turned to a scowl. "You have no idea what happens out there, outside the safe confines of our protected planet and the shiny lie of a life you live. Out there, all these niceties and titles don't mean anything. Everyone back here is just a prisoner of your delusions."

"I'm not the one living a lie, Emily," snapped back Aria. "You talk down on the very society you claim to fight for and treat everyone here like they are less than you because they want security … security you so proudly claim to provide. So you spout on about your defense of the Humani people and then look down on us for enjoying it … that's very convenient, Paladin Martin. You put on this big show when I think you're actually afraid of having to live with real people because you'll see just how much your hatred for the First Families and the constant violence of your life has changed you. I wonder if you're even the same species anymore."

Martin felt her muscles tighten and her teeth clench. She knew Aria was a social-climbing opportunist — like all good Humani — but the logic of her cousin's honest, albeit misguided, argument frustrated her. And the fact Martin knew the real truth about the Humani civilization only added salt to wound Aria had opened.

"Real people," guffawed Martin. "The real people are the ones out there dying for you so that you can have this fancy, overpriced meal." She felt her body growing hot, and despite her efforts to stop it, a tear rolled down her cheek. "I've seen Guardsmen's bodies laid open …" She paused again as the scenes from that horrible mission on Golf 2 washed over her body. "… dying for a fucking lie. And some of them were because of that son-of-bitch Sequentis Varus. He's lucky I didn't end him right there at the table … like I should have years ago," she added, looking directly into the wide eyes of her cousin.

"How can you talk about killing someone so easily? Doesn't it bother you?"

"Not the ones that have it coming."

"That's what I mean; you just —"

"Seriously, Aria — this whole society is built on a foundation of blood, and you want me to feel bad for spilling it when all of you bathe in it daily?"

"What are you talking about?"

"I've seen horrible things, Aria … done horrible things." She froze again as the dirty face of a blonde-haired Phelian girl flashed in her mind. She closed her eyes as she felt the sensation of pulling the trigger of the gun that took her life. She opened her eyes. "But this place disgusts me even more."

"This was a mistake," said Aria. "I just thought it would be nice to talk to my cousin … the one I played with as a child."

"She doesn't exist anymore."

"Even so," replied Aria. "You have to understand what your new title can do for you … for the whole family."

And there it was. She was acting as the instrument of the Martin family, hoping to capitalize on her new position and notoriety. Martin rose from the table.

"I'm sorry, Aria. I know it's not your fault. You're just playing the role you were taught to play."

"And you, Paladin Martin … aren't you just playing a role," shot back Aria. "Paladin Emily Martin, the hot-headed, belligerent soldier. You had it rough as a kid, your mom left, and your father's a drunk that —"

Martin's vision tunneled and a bolt of rage surged through her body. She stepped toward Aria, who stopped mid-sentence, leaning backwards in her chair.

"Never," spoke Martin through her teeth. "Never speak of her." She could feel her body shaking as she put her hands on the table and leaned in too close to Aria. "And if you want to finish what you were going to say about my father?"

Aria sat silently, avoiding eye contact with her.

"You people are mindless sheep following a corrupt shepherd you can't even see."

"And what does that make you?" asked Aria, slowly looking toward Martin.

Martin could see the disgust on her cousin's face.

"That, my dear cousin Aria, makes me the wolf." She stood erect. "But don't worry, I'm not hunting sheep … I'm going after the shepherd."

"What are you talking about?"

"You just enjoy your dinner, cousin," she replied, pulling a credit chip from her pocket and tossing it on the table. "Just have them send my steak to the bar," she added as she turned to walk away.

She paused after a few steps, turning back toward Aria. "Oh, and you can tell the Martin patriarchs to go fuck themselves."

Chapter 8

Martin let out a frustrated puff of air as she stood on the platform outside Primum. She knew her cousin couldn't help being the way she was; she was just another unknowing pawn in the façade created by the Xen and perpetuated by the First Families. Hopefully all of that would change, but only if she —

"Emily!"

Martin's thoughts were interrupted by a shout from her cousin. She looked down to see Aria standing at the edge of the platform.

"What is it, Aria?" she asked with a sigh.

"I just didn't want to leave things like that. I —"

Martin's attention was drawn from her cousin to two men standing several meters behind Aria on the lower platform. While everyone pushed their way through and around others on the platform, they stood dead still in the center of the crowd. Staring at each other, the two men wore coats too heavy for the mild season. And their hair styles — shoulder length in the back with two tufts running down their cheeks.

"No … not here," she mouthed. "Aria, get up here."

"What … did you even hear —"

"Aria, just shut up and get up here," she ordered, extending her hand.

"Fine," replied Aria, grasping Martin's hand.

Martin hefted Aria onto the upper platform, catching a glimpse of a man and a woman, similar in dress and appearance to the two men, step onto the upper platform a few meters away. They were met instantly by a constable.

"You two cannot be up here," he ordered.

The man and woman looked at each other and then returned a blank stare to the constable. Martin saw the undeniable look of determination in their eyes. "Damn it," she cursed, drawing her pistol as she pushed Aria behind her. "Constable! Stop them!" she shouted.

The constable turned toward the sound of Martin's voice. As he did, the man drew a pistol and swung it toward the constable's head.

Martin raised her weapon and fired two quick rounds, knocking both the man and the woman to the ground as chaos enveloped the platform and the walkway below. "Call for backup!" she ordered, swinging her pistol toward the two men on the commoner walkway. As she did, one of the men raised his arms into the air, exposing an explosive device strapped to his chest.

"For the Saint!" the follower shouted before detonating the explosive.

Martin fell to the ground, dragging Aria with her. The blast rocked Martin to her bones and forced the air from her lungs. Rolling onto her back, she took in a quick forced breath and sprung to her knees.

She looked where the two men had stood.

The scene was gruesome. Martin saw the dead and dying scattered across the walkway. The ringing in her ears subsided and was replaced by screams of terror and agony from the wrecked pile of flesh below her.

"Son of a bitch!" she cursed, scanning the area for more threats. Seeing no more, she turned back toward the constable. Although a stream of blood trickled down his temple, he had recovered and was moving toward the two people on the upper platform Martin had shot.

"Did you get the report out?" asked Martin, rising to her feet.

"Yes," he replied. "What —"

Martin saw the wounded woman roll onto her back, exposing another explosive device.

"G —"

Before she could speak, another blast ripped through the upper platform, engulfing the constable in ball of fire and knocking Martin back onto the ground. Her face burning from the heat of the blast, she let out a heavy grunt and pushed herself back to her feet. Dozens of Humani, commoner and First Family alike, lay scattered in all directions. Others huddled together in small groups while a few sat on the ground, frozen by shock and fear.

Martin looked back toward the first explosion. She saw a man trying to apply pressure to a woman's — probably his wife's — severed leg. Another limped into view, bleeding from a mangled left arm.

"Help me," he pleaded to anyone that could hear before collapsing onto the ground.

"Aria," she said aloud and turned toward where her cousin had been.

Aria was curled into a tight ball, her hands covering her head. "Aria? Are you okay?" she asked, placing her hand on her cousin's shoulder.

Gently pulling her cousin's hand from her face and rolling her on her back, Martin checked her for injuries. She was shaking uncontrollably but didn't seem to be injured.

"You're okay, Aria," said Martin.

"What … what happened?" stammered Aria. "I —"

"This is the reality I was talking about, cousin," replied Martin. "It looks like the Dark Zone has finally come to Alpha Humana. We are finally going to reap what we have sown there for generations."

"What?"

"And there will be more," said Martin.

***

Summoned to a meeting of Astra Varus's private council, Martin found herself surrounded by Senators Sarius and Lucretia, General Vispa, and Chief Magistrate of Mt. Castra, Gal Solara.

"Here!" shouted Astra. "On Alpha Humana!"

"Yes, ProConsul," replied Martin. "I was there. They were followers of the Word … of the Saint, no doubt. Several were killed and more severely injured."

"Were any First Family members injured?" asked Astra.

Martin clinched her teeth. "I didn't take the time to ask their family status while I was trying to keep their guts from falling out … ProConsul."

"How did this happen?" asked Astra, ignoring Martin's response as she turned to the Chief Magistrate Solara.

"We have not yet had time to answer that question, ProConsul," replied Solara. "The investigatory capabilities of my department under the current budget are —"

Martin guffawed.

"What is it, Paladin?" said Astra. "Is there something funny about an attack on our home planet?"

"No, ProConsul," replied Martin. "I've sworn my life to defend the Humani people against any threat … external or internal." She continued, pointing toward Chief Magistrate Solara. "What's funny is this guy beating around the bush. He knows — just like every other First Family member, military officer, lawman, and trader — that people are constantly being brought here from the Dark Zone to be servants in the recreation houses and homes of the First Families. It's a direct line to the heart of Humani leadership … via their own lazy, lecherous, and vain lifestyle."

"How dare you!" shot back Solara.

"How dare I?" replied Martin. "You pompous ass … there are dead Humani laying in the streets and you're fucking trying to get more credits for your department. Here's an idea … just do your damn job."

Martin turned from Solara toward Astra. She could see Astra's face twisted in frustration. Astra Varus was a lot of things, but she wasn't a fool, and the implications of the elite's labor force turning on the First Families clearly unsettled her.

"Magistrate Solara," said Astra. "What is your plan?"

"Well, ProConsul, once we have —"

"Now!" screamed Astra, her voice cracking with anger as she slammed her fist into the arm of her chair. "What is your plan right now?"

"Yes, ProConsul," stammered Solara. "I will halt the influx of laborers to Mt. Castra from the Neutral Quadrant with the physical descriptions matching those of the attackers from today."

"And you think they will not alter their appearance once they know we are looking for them?" asked Astra.

Martin could see the frustration grow on Astra's face.

"General Vispa," continued Astra, "what are your recommendations?"

"This is a problem well beyond the capabilities of civilian authorities," replied Vispa with a glance toward Solara. "Even if we stop the influx from Mt. Castra, that does not mean they cannot enter through another city … or that others aren't already here or in other cities."

"Then all of the First Families are at risk?" posed Senator Marcus Sarius.

"As well as the rest of the Humani people," replied Martin, staring down the Senator. "They might not like getting blown apart by lunatics either."

"Of course," replied the Senator. "But the threat to the First Families is immediate and must be prioritized."

"Because you have to have your asses wiped by stables of servants," spat Martin.

"Paladin Martin!" shouted the Senator. "Do not forget your place."

"I haven't … maybe you shouldn't forget what I am capable of," she said with a smile.

"Enough!" shouted Astra. Rising from her chair, the ProConsul walked to the center of the group. "Magistrate Solara, as of this moment your department will fall under the authority of Humani High Command."

"But —"

Astra raised her hand to silence the Solara. "As will all civilian enforcement officers in every city."

"Martial law?" asked Senator Lucretia.

"Imperial law," replied Astra.

Martin's draw dropped. Astra Varus was using an attack on her own people, one ultimately caused by her own scheming, to make her final move for total power.

"This is a critical time," continued Astra, her eyes electric, "and we must take decisive action." She turned slowly and ascended the steps to her chair. At her chair, she turned and sat slowly, the room silent as everyone waited for her next words.

"General Vispa and Magistrate Solara, pass the word through secure channels that all civil enforcement authorities are to immediately fall under the direction of regional military commanders. They are to provide detailed reports on their strength as well as possible

threats to the region commander in five standard
hours. The regional commanders will then report
to you, General Vispa, within ten hours. Also
pass the word on to all combatant commanders."

"Yes, ProConsul," replied Vispa and Solara
in unison.

"Senator Sarius, prepare the following media
link and inform the media department I will
address the Humani people in twenty-four hours.
The link will say …" Astra activated the
recording device on her chair and continued:

"Many of you have heard of the attack on
our defenseless civilians that occurred yesterday
in our capitol. Despite the deadly intent of the
attackers, the impact was limited by the bravery
of our hero Paladin Martin and the Mt. Castra
constable force. Further investigation has
determined that the attack was planned and
carried out by Terillian operatives that were able
to infiltrate our home world, most likely with the
help of the Traitor, Tyler Stone."

Martin's stomach churned as she listened to
Astra spin the web of lies she would use to
achieve ultimate, uncontested power.

Astra continued.

"We have also learned that other terrorists
may be in route or are already on our planet.
With the security of the Humani people in mind,
I have implemented the following directive …"

Here it comes, thought Martin, almost
physically ill.

"… All Humani civil authorities have been placed under direction of regional military commanders to ensure the broadest sharing of intelligence and resources as well as providing the highest level of protection for our facilities, institutions, and people. With the Terillian threat now facing us on our home soil, I am also forced to take the drastic, but necessary action of temporarily limiting the political power of the Senate. This measure, while unprecedented in our history, is fully supported by the Patrician Council and key members of Senate. It is done so that I may quickly and decisively respond to threats to the Humani people as they occur …"

Martin thought of her cousin. *They are going to lap this up*, she realized, closing her eyes.

"… As our brave warriors face the Terillian hordes in the Neutral Quadrant, we must likewise be prepared to do the same on our home soil to protect ourselves — our families and our way of life, as well — from those that would destroy it and enslave us."

Martin had to turn away. Rage and disgust overwhelmed her. Martial law was going to make her mission even more difficult.

"There," ended Astra. "Have this played on all media links in fifteen hours, but first make sure the attack is the top story until then. Include multiple speculative reports on the cause and the groups possibly behind it. Include possible dissident groups within our society and government. Also play up the possibility of other attacks."

"Yes, ProConsul," replied Senator Sarius with a smile. "Some senators will resist," he added.

"Then they will be labeled as enemies of the Humani people," replied Astra. "We will show the people what fear feels like, and they will beg for security …" Astra paused. "Which we will provide."

"Yes, ProConsul," said Sarius. "We must also discuss implications for other initiatives."

Martin's ears perked. Sarius had slipped up. She knew he had to be talking about the plans for Dolus.

"That," replied Astra, shooting daggers through Sarius with her eyes, "is for another time."

"Yes, ProConsul," said Sarius, his voice muted.

"Now," continued Astra, "are there any questions?"

"No, ProConsul," echoed the group.

"Very well, then. Let us get to work. General Vispa and Senator Sarius, remain behind please."

"Yes, ProConsul," they responded.

"And Paladin Martin —"

"Yes, ProConsul," replied Martin flatly.

"Find Stone."

"Yes, ProConsul." Martin snapped to attention and gave a rigid salute. She yearned for the day she would be able to wrap her hands around the throat of that tyrannical bitch. But for now she would have to play along.

***

Martin and the others having left her chambers, Astra turned toward Senator Sarius.

"ProConsul, I would like to —"

Astra focused the full force of her body into her hand as she slapped the Senator across the face mid-sentence. "I will not tolerate a fool, Senator," scolded Astra. "Speak without thinking again and you may find yourself labeled an enemy of the people and shipped off to Capro prison."

"It will not happen again, ProConsul," replied Sarius, his head looking toward the floor.

"You are right, Senator. It will not."

"Might I say, ProConsul," added Senator Lucretia, "that was a brilliant move—utilizing the attack to further consolidate your power. That will allow us to significantly increase the resources put toward Dolus."

"It will," replied Astra, "but we must deal with these Followers."

"Once the military has assumed control, we will begin reviewing records of all servants. I will assign units to identify anyone, regardless of class, thought to be involved in suspicious activity or that have originated from areas where there is support for the Word movement. They will be segregated and then interrogated," said Vispa.

"Very well, General Vispa," said Astra. "But we must also look into the possible threats from groups resistant to my authority."

"Of course, ProConsul. These groups are well documented, but we will increase surveillance and put pressure on their leadership. Now that I have control of the magistrate, I will use them, as well, by appointing military courts in place of civilian ones in cases of possible sedition or treason."

Astra leaned back, her hands gripping the arms of her chair. She let out a long, comfortable breath. "Now all I need is for that rabid, insubordinate bitch Martin to bring me Stone's head on a platter so I can rid myself of her as well."

Chapter 9

"Attention!" shouted a lieutenant as Stone walked into Colonel Vae's command post.

"At ease," ordered Stone.

"Good afternoon, Sir," said Vae. "Welcome to 1st Brigade's command post."

"Nice to see you, Colonel. I thought I would come by for a sitrep and to see your operation."

"Of course," replied Vae, walking to a digital map at a nearby table. "We've overseen the emigration of approximately fifteen thousand into the protected cities —"

"Approximately?" asked Stone.

"Sorry, Sir. Fifteen thousand, two hundred ninety-three have moved through our lines in two standard months as of this morning's reports. We have stopped two hundred four possible insurgents with one hundred forty confirmed to be Followers of the Word."

"And attacks?"

"We have experienced fifteen attacks on our boundary locations, ten of which have been suicide attacks. We have also responded to eight requests for support from local authorities in the interior."

"I am aware of the attacks in the cities," replied Stone. "And your prompt responses have saved lives."

"Thank you, Sir. It seems, despite the attacks, the cities are functioning."

"Functioning, but on edge," replied Stone. "I've spoken with local authorities and they fear more agents are in the cities and plotting larger attacks."

"I can provide a company to assist —"

"Thank you, Colonel, but this mission calls for special-operations-capable troops."

"The Scout Rangers?" asked Vae.

"Yes, I received word this morning a unit had arrived in orbit. I have asked them to meet here, as your intelligence files are the most in-depth in regard to attempted infiltrations. Once they review the data, I'll have them meet with the local leaders' security officers."

"Do you know who will be leading them?"

"I do not; I made the request through Akota command and it was granted by the Shirt-Wearers, but the response only stated that a unit would be dispatched."

"How has Scarus and 1st Brigade been doing?"

"They've made progress but it's slow going," replied Stone. "He has taken some casualties and a few villages have still been caught in the middle." Stone paused. "How is your unit dealing with Maxa's removal?"

"My senior officers have reported the occasional dust-up, but no events of mutiny or even significant disruptions … just talk, mostly."

"We must keep an eye on it, Colonel," warned Stone. "The last thing we need is a revolt within our own ranks."

"Of course, Sir," replied Vae. "I have —"

The green light above the entrance to Colonel Vae's command post illuminated.

"What is it? I am with the General," demanded Vae.

"*The Scout Ranger commander has arrived, Sir,*" came a voice through the intercom.

Vae looked up toward Stone, who responded with a nod.

"Let them in," replied Vae.

Stone turned toward the door as it slid open. Standing at the entrance was a pair of brilliant green eyes staring back at him.

"Mor … Major Skye," stammered Stone. "I thought you were —"

"We rotated out of the invasion training, General," replied Mori. "So the Shirt-Wearers directed my battalion be sent to support you."

Stone stood silent, his gaze still focused on Mori. Although her face was not painted, she was in full combat gear and her hair was tied in the familiar braided tails she wore into battle. He wanted to speak but couldn't form the words.

Seconds seemed like minutes as the two stared at one another.

"General, Sir," spoke Vae, breaking the silence. "Perhaps we should discuss the tactical situation?"

"Yes, of course," answered Stone. "Major Skye, your Rangers will be very helpful here. Although we've reduced number of attacks in the cities and pushed the Followers back in this region, we are still seeing attacks in the area. I want your troops to carry out raids against suspected insurgent strongholds within the city. Colonel Vae can provide a good overview of security issues as well as details on insurgent weapons and tactics. When you are done with the Colonel, the local security officers for Inotib, Ezah, Elleb, Nager, and Arerrac will provide intel on the suspected locations of trouble spots. After that, you will carry out raids on these locations, minimizing civilian casualties whenever possible."

"Perhaps, General, we should speak first," said Mori, her eyes wide and mouth slack. "We have —"

"Yes ... I ..." Stone didn't know how much Vae knew about his relationship with Mori and he didn't want the first meeting between one of his brigade commanders and the leader of the special operations teams to be unprofessional. "I want to make sure you are up to speed on the tactical situation before we discuss other issues."

"Other issues?" guffawed Mori. "Is that …" She paused. "Yes, Major General Stone. When I am fully briefed, I will schedule a meeting through your staff."

"Major, I …" Stone suddenly realized how Humani — and un-Akota — he had treated Mori. "I didn't mean to … I was —"

"If that's all, Sir," interrupted Mori. "I should get to work. That is why I am here, isn't it, Sir?"

He could see he had hurt her … again. "Mori … Ino'ka —" He paused, realizing he had used her Akota name in front of a Humani, a betrayal of privacy to the Akota. "I'm —"

"If that is all, Sir?" interrupted Mori, her eyes full of pain and frustration.

"Yes," he replied, trying to convey his regret about his actions. "We'll talk later."

***

Stone slouched in the chair at his desk, swirling a half-empty glass of whiskey in his hand. He closed his eyes and exhaled deeply. "Stupid," he said aloud, thinking of how he had treated Mori earlier. Another deep breath, and he pulled a status report from his desk. He started to read the report, but his thoughts drifted to first time he had encountered the Followers. He saw the innocent look on the young girl's face as he pulled the trigger and she fell.

He took another drink. The warm sting of the alcohol tracing its way through his body did little to counter the chill running down his spine. Taking another drink, he slouched back into his chair. Exhausted from the day and his past, Stone drifted off to sleep.

The buzz of someone at his door startled him. Jumping to his feet, the remaining alcohol spilled onto the floor and Stone's trousers. "Damn it," he cursed, patting at his leg. "Come in," he ordered.

The door slid open and a pair of familiar green eyes stared back at him.

"Ino'ka!" he almost shouted. "I … I'm glad to see you."

"I finished going over the intel with your Colonel Vae and just needed to —"

"Yes," replied Stone, eager to make up for earlier. "I —"

The impact of Mori's open hand across his cheek silenced him.

"I just needed to tell you you're a son-of-a-bitch," snapped Mori.

"I'm sorry, Ino'ka," he replied, his jaw stinging. "I —"

"First, you treat me like a stranger … then you say my Akota name in front of a … a Hanmani." She grasped his shirt, pulling him toward her. "What's happened to you?"

"I don't want to hurt you. I —"

"Well, you did. Do you know what it felt like …?" She paused, clinching her teeth. "… what it feels like to see the man you love after months and to be treated like …" She paused again. "Or is that the way you want it to be?"

"No," replied Stone. "Don't you think I wanted to take you in my arms the second I saw you?"

"Then why didn't you?"

"I … the Humani officers aren't used to displays …" He paused, letting out a frustrated breath. "It's complicated."

"Well it shouldn't be. And that's the problem."

"Ino'ka," replied Stone, stepping close to Mori and gripping her arms tightly. "I need these men to follow me … what we are doing here is important."

"You think I don't know that," replied Mori. "But you don't have to be —"

"They aren't Akota; they're Humani. And they need to know they are being led by a Humani."

Mori stepped back, breaking Stone's hold. "So you're turning your back on —"

"I'm not turning my back on anything. I'm trying to lead these men and keep as many of them alive as possible while stopping this planet from falling into the hands of the Word." He grabbed her arms again, pulling her toward him. "Just because I acted formally when we met doesn't mean I don't love you, Ino'ka. I'm playing the role I need to in order to accomplish the mission."

"Playing a role," huffed Mori. "A leader leads and their troops follow. If you are playing a role, then they are following a lie. An Akota would not —"

"They're not Akota," growled Stone. He exhaled, lightening his grip on Mori's arms. "That's the point. I can't treat these men like Akota, just like I wouldn't treat Akota soldiers like Humani."

"Well … I …" Mori looked down at the floor briefly before looking back up toward Stone. "I don't know what to think anymore. First, you take this command without even discussing it with me. Then, I barely hear from you all this time. And then …" she paused, "… you treat me like a stranger."

"I have to keep my professional and personal lives separate when I'm —"

"Separate?" interrupted Mori. "How is that even possible? An Akota —"

"I'm not Akota!" shouted Stone.

Mori stepped away from Stone.

"I mean, I'm not all … damn it," cursed Stone. "You can't expect me to just forget about my life before I met you."

"I know what you meant," replied Mori flatly. "You're still lost, and working with these Hanmani is only making it worse."

"I'm helping these people. Can't you see that?"

"And losing yourself," replied Mori.

Stone looking into Mori's beautiful green eyes. He knew his words would hurt, but he needed her to understand. "I've felt more like myself for the last few months than I have in a long time."

"I see," replied Mori, slightly nodding her head as tears began to roll down her cheeks.

"No, you don't," said Stone. "I'm not saying I don't love you and don't want to be with you … I'm just saying I can't become something I'm not."

"It's not becoming something you're not … it's becoming what you were meant to be."

"And if I dealt with these men like Akota, this mission would fail and the Word would sweep over this planet," retorted Stone. "Is that what you want?"

"I want you," she replied. "We are meant to —"

"I can't live my life based on a dream," interrupted Stone. "I have to do what is best for the most people, and sometimes that doesn't fit perfectly into what you've envisioned for our future, Ino'ka. And do you think the Shirt-Wearers would have given me this command if it didn't fit into the Akota agenda?"

"I don't … I … damn it!" cursed Mori. "Why does this have to be so hard?"

"You mean a relationship between a Humani First Family officer who turned against his government and the only female Ka-itsenko?" posed Stone. "Nothing about our relationship is, or should be, easy, Ino'ka," he continued with a smile as he again stepped toward her. "It's hard … but it has to be." He pulled her head into her chest. "Do you love me?" he asked, placing his hand on her head.

"Yes," she answered, wrapping her arms around his waist. "But it —"

"And I love you," he replied, moving her shoulders back so he could look into her eyes. "But it's not going to be easy … and I will make mistakes." He placed his hand on her cheek. "A lot of them."

"Just don't forget at your core, you're Akota, Magakisca," she replied, placing her hands on his cheeks. "They all are lost Akota, and you can help them find themselves …" Mori's hands tightened around his face. "… If you don't allow yourself to get drawn back into a past that is a lie. Your future, and ours, lies in what can be — not in what has been."

"I will try," he replied. "But you must also let me lead these men the way I see fit … and understand they don't think like Akota."

"I'll be a good ozuye," she replied, using the Akota word for warrior. "And follow your orders," she smiled.

He leaned down to kiss Mori.

Stone stumbled and fell into the couch by his desk as Mori pushed him backwards. Her weight pressed down on his waist as she straddled him.

"But tonight, General," she smiled, undoing the belt holding her sword and sidearm. "You belong to me," she added, unbuttoning his tunic.

"Yes, ma'am," replied Stone, his hands sliding from Mori's face to the buttons on her uniform. "You don't know how long I've been waiting to touch you," he said.

"Yes I do," she replied. "Now shut up, soldier, and take off my shirt."

"Yes ma'am —"

The light above Stone's door buzzed green and a young lieutenant burst through the door as it slid open.

"What are you doing, lieutenant?" shouted Stone, rising as Mori jumped to her feet.

"General … I …" The young officer paused, seeing Stone and Mori standing next to each other, both their uniforms partially undone. "I didn't …"

"What is it?" demanded Stone, buttoning his shirt.

"Uh, yes, Sir," stammered the officer. "We just received word of another attack, this time at the main civilian security offices in Inotib." He paused again. "I'm sorry, but you did not have the 'No Entry' light on … and you said to report any major attacks in the —"

"Yes, Lieutenant," replied Stone. "Notify the rest of my staff and I want a transport ready in ten minutes." He looked toward Mori, who seemed more annoyed than embarrassed. But she wasn't Humani. "Major, I would like you to join me."

"Maj —," Mori paused, her frustration clearly growing. "Of course, General," the words shot out like bullets. "I will have your staff give me the location of your transport," she added, grabbing her service belt, which held her sword and sidearm. "Now, if I may be excused?" she added, snapping to attention and saluting before turning and storming out of the room, almost knocking the lieutenant off balance.

"I'm sorry, Sir," offered the lieutenant.

"You're fine, Lieutenant," replied Stone. He had no idea if Mori was pissed about the interruption or about him calling her by her rank. But Stone was sure he would find out soon enough. "Let's go," ordered Stone, grabbing his belt.

"Do you have early casualty reports?" Stone asked his aid, adjusting his holster while hustling toward the transport.

"Incomplete, but at least fifteen, Sir."

"Is the scene secure?"

"Colonel Vae reports local security forces have set up a perimeter and he has dispatched a platoon of infantry to support."

Two soldiers and a captain standing at the
entrance to Stone's transport came to attention
and saluted.

"At ease," ordered Stone as he stepped
inside his transport.

"We are ready to launch, General," said the
captain, following Stone inside. "I and a squad of
my men will be providing security for you."

"Security?" Stone heard Mori's voice.

Stone turned to see Mori and two Scout
Ranger officers standing at the entrance, her face
now painted in red and yellow diagonal stripes
covering her face, with a black handprint
covering her lower jaw.

"Of course, Major," replied the Humani
captain, his eyes wide as he took in Mori's
warpaint; it was clearly the first time he had seen
a painted-face warrior. "All flag officers receive a
security detachment when traveling into possibly
hazardous areas."

"A warrior doesn't need … what did you
call it … a security detachment?" replied Mori.

"But Major, it's the regulations —"

"It's okay, Captain," interrupted Stone.
"Akota warriors have different practices than the
Humani."

"Yeah," replied Mori, stepping close to the
captain. "Akota officers don't need protection,"
she continued, looking over the captain's
shoulder directly into Stone's eyes.

"Nor do Humani," replied the captain, drawing Mori's gaze again. "But we do show respect and concern for our superiors."

Mori's green eyes burned holes through the Humani captain, her jaw clinched tightly.

"I think we have discussed this enough," said Stone, breaking the tense silence. "We need to get to the scene." He depressed the intercom on the bulkhead. "We're ready for takeoff," he said.

The transport shuddered as it lifted off the platform.

"Orders, Sir?" asked the captain, turning away from Mori.

"Join your men in the ready compartment, Captain," replied Stone. "I'll want them to set up a perimeter around the transport when we land, and you will join me."

"Yes, Sir," replied the captain with a salute before exiting the compartment.

"Lieutenant," continued Stone. "Go along with the captain and get yourself a rifle."

"Yes, Sir," replied the aid.

"And Lieutenant," added Stone. "Get one for me as well."

"Yes, Sir," said the aid before he scurried off to join the captain.

Stone and Mori sat alone at his desk, neither speaking. After a few moments of the nothing but the hum of engines, Mori spoke.

"Seriously," she laughed. "Do you have someone to help you wipe your —"

"That's enough!" interrupted Stone. "You said you'd do your duty."

"And I will," snapped Mori. "Point me at the enemy and I'll kill them."

"Can you not antagonize my officers … please?"

"Fine," replied Mori. "I should've known better than to try to understand Hanmani behavior."

"Just let me deal with my men, and I will point you at the enemy soon enough."

"Yes, Sir," she replied, giving a sarcastic salute while sitting across from Stone.

"Mori, I need you to do this."

"Fine. I'll leave your little minions alone," she condeded.

"General, Sir," said the aid as he entered the compartment, an assault rifle in each hand. "Sorry for the interruption, but —"

"You're very good at it, Lieutenant," interrupted Mori with a laugh.

"Continue, Lieutenant Sandis," said Stone with a frustrated glance toward Mori.

"Yes, Sir," continued the aid, giving a rifle and ammunition to Stone. "I have your weapon and three magazines. Captain Larson also reports that his men are standing by."

"Very well, Lieutenant," replied Stone, placing the additional magazines in his pockets.

"Is this gonna be a hot landing?" asked Mori.

"We should have a secure landing site," replied Stone. "But we won't really know for sure until we hit the ground."

"Be ready to fight," Mori said in Akota to the two officers with her. "But only take out clear targets … no civilian casualties."

Both officers acknowledged her in Akota.

"And keep your eyes on these Hanmani … I have no idea what they'll do if it gets hot," she added.

"They'll do fine," grumbled Stone, also in Akota. "Just worry about your warriors."

"Standby for landing in three minutes," came over the intercom circuit.

"I don't have to worry about them, Magakisca," replied Mori. "I just don't want your men getting mine killed."

"If you trust me, then you trust them," replied Stone slowly.

"Then I guess we have nothing to worry about," said Mori in Humani. "Let's get to it."

The increased noise of the engines told Stone the transport was coming into a hover, and a slight flutter in his stomach told him the descent had begun. "Let's get to the entrance," he ordered.

Chapter 10

A group of Humani troops rushed past Mori as the hatch to the transport opened. She turned to see Stone step forward, but Captain Larson placed his arm on his shoulder to hold him back.

"Sir, wait for the perimeter," said Larson.

She could see the frustration on Stone's face and it brought a satisfying smile to her own.

"It's just the landing site, Captain," replied Stone as he stepped past Larson, "I'll be fine."

"Yes, Sir," conceded Larson.

"Nice try," said Mori, patting Captain Larson on the shoulder as she followed Stone through the exit.

Once outside, she noticed three light hover tanks and two armored hovercraft in front of the transport. As the protection platoon scattered out around the transport, Mori and her officers followed Stone and his entourage to the convoy.

Another Humani officer standing at the first hovercraft saluted as Stone approached.

"At ease, Captain," said Stone, returning the salute. "What is the status?"

"The scene is a few blocks away and appears to be secure. I have two platoons providing roving patrols in support of the local security forces who have set up the perimeter."

"It's still a mess over there," added Colonel Vae as he exited the lead hovercraft. "We are up to twenty-three killed and probably over one hundred injured … about half are civilians."

"Let's go take a look," said Stone. "Captain, you and Lieutenant Sandis take the second hovercraft." He turned toward Mori. "I want you to join the Colonel and me," he said. "Can your officers ride with my staff?"

"Do we need an interpreter?" asked Larson.

"We speak Humani," replied one of the officers. "All Scout Ranger officers know the language of their enemy."

Larson and the officer returned a long silent stare.

"Well then, I guess they don't need one," said Mori, breaking the silence. "Go with the captain, brothers." She paused. "Maybe you can teach them our alphabet on the way," she added in Akota with a smile, knowing Stone was the only non-Scout Ranger to understand it.

"Let's go," ordered Stone with a scowl.

Mori placed one foot onto the access ladder and pulled herself into the open-top hovercraft. Inside the troop compartment, she glanced into the control cockpit. Staring back at her was the young driver, his eyes wide. Mori realized it was probably the first time most of Stone's men had seen a Scout Ranger, and definitely the first time he had seen a Ka-itsenko in full combat dress. "Boo!" she shouted, and the driver quickly turned back to his controls. Letting out a small chuckle, Mori sat next to Stone.

"Having fun, Ino'ka?" whispered Stone in Akota.

"A little," she replied.

"Are you ready, Sir?" asked Vae, stepping into the troop compartment.

"Yes, Colonel."

"Driver, notify the convoy to move," ordered Vae.

Mori heard the engines rev and felt her body shift as the hovercraft began to move. With the tanks in front and the rear, the convoy picked up speed and headed toward the scene of the attack. Turning the first corner, Mori saw a line of medical and emergency vehicles parked along the street as people streamed away from the scene. Looking over the side of the hovercraft, she saw a local security checkpoint wave the convoy through. "Colonel Vae, are the perimeters controlled only on the streets?"

"I recommended to the locals that they control access through the buildings and underground, as well," replied Vae, "but I doubt they have all areas covered. As I mentioned, I deployed a platoon split up into squads to patrol likely weak spots."

Mori looked toward Stone. She could see he understood.

"What do you want?" he asked.

"I want my officers to cover from above," she replied.

Stone activated the hovercraft internal communications system. "Driver, patch us in to the second hovercraft."

"Yes, Sir," replied the driver. "Mantis 2, this is Mantis 1; standby for message," he alerted on the intercom. "You're patched in, Sir."

Stone motioned for Mori to speak.

Mori leaned over to the intercom. "Brothers, this is Ino'ka," she spoke in Akota. "Deploy here and cover blast site from the rooftops."

Stone activated his comms device. "I'll oder the convoy stopped so they can —"

"*Mantis 1, this is Mantis 2*," broke over the circuit. "*Those Terillians just jumped out of the hovercraft!*"

"We don't need to stop, Colonel," replied Stone with a smile toward Mori.

A few short moments later, the convoy came to a halt.

Mori jumped out of the hovercraft onto the hard pavement below. She quickly took in the scene. Spotlights and flames broke through the dark night, illuminating the chaos all around her. To her left was a triage station where medics hurried back and forth, trying to tend to the wounded and gather information. Behind the triage station, she saw dozens of bodies covered with orange blankets. She glanced to the right, where a number of local security officers and a few Humani officers were gathered behind a thin line of security troops. Directly in front of her lay the remains of a three-story brick building. The front end of the structure had collapsed, and flames rose from both the rubble and the rear of the building as firefighters and rescue personnel fought to control the blaze and find survivors.

"The incident command is over there," said Vae, pointing to the group of officers.

"*Captain Rain, in position*," Mori heard one of her officers report through her comms link.

"*Captain Springfall, in position to the North*," came a second report.

"Keep your eyes and ears open," she replied, scanning the area intently.

"Do you need more support?" asked Stone.

"We have other units standing by to help," replied Vae, "but more people here would just get in the way."

"And security around the area?" asked Mori. "Any concerns for secondary explosions?"

"We think if they had secondary detonations planned, they would have already set them off. We also have teams out using both electronic and canine detection … we have found nothing so far."

"I want to talk to the senior security officer," said Stone.

"*Movement in third story window one hundred fifty meters west of your location,*" reported Captain Rain.

"Movement over there," reported Mori. "Third floor," she added, pointing toward a building behind the group of officers. "What do you see?" she spoke into her comms link. "Let me —"

Mori saw a green laser flicker off the button on Stone's uniform. "Sniper!" she yelled.

Before she could reach the two, Larson stepped in front of Stone, a bullet tearing into his back almost instantly.

"Take cover!" shouted Vae. Rescue workers and soldiers scattered as the crack of the Akota officers' weapons return fire echoed through the street.

Mori slid to her knees beside Stone just as he was rolling the body of Captain Larson off of him. "You okay?" shouted Mori, her rifle trained on the building.

"Yeah, I'm — damn it," cursed Stone, looking down toward Larson.

Mori looked down at Captain Larson. The bullet had pierced his back and tore through his chest. Her heart stopped as she glanced toward Stone. His uniform was covered in blood. "Are you hit?" she shouted, running her hand over the blood on his shirt. As she did, she saw a bullet fragment fall from his combat vest.

"I'm okay!" shouted Stone. "Did we get the shooter?"

"Did you get him?" said Mori into her comms link.

"*Target down,*" reported Rain. "*In route to confirm.*"

"Are you okay, Sir?" asked Vae.

"Yes," replied Stone, picking up his rifle. "I want to see the sniper."

"My men are already on the way," said Mori.

"Let's go," said Stone, starting toward the building.

"Status," ordered Mori into her comms link.

"*We're in the room. No shooter, but we have blood, a rifle, and an empty coagulate applicator,*" came the report.

"Damn it," replied Mori. "Shooter's gone."

"Son of a bitch," cursed Stone.

"This doesn't seem right," posed Mori. "A sniper from that distance was unlikely to cause as much damage as another explosion or an overt, close-up attack."

"Doesn't seem like a move the Followers would make, does it?" added Stone.

"A sniper is a needle … the Word uses hammers," replied Mori. "And apparently that needle was pointed at you."

"They could be focusing on leadership and using a bombing to draw out high-ranking officers," said Stone.

"You do realize most high-ranking officers wouldn't show up to a bombing, right?" replied Mori. "But you would …"

"What is it?"

Mori grabbed Stone's arm. "Do you have any enemies here other than Followers? Is there any chance the Humani or Xen know you're here?"

"I doubt they know I'm here, but it's not impossible," replied Stone. He paused, giving a knowing glance toward Vae. "Maxa …"

"Who?"

"Can your men keep on his trail if the shooter's stopped bleeding?" asked Stone.

Mori curled her lip, smirking at Stone. "Stay on the shooter," she ordered into her comms circuit. "Now who is this Maxa?"

"There was a former warlord from the Dark Zone in charge of one of my brigades when I took command. We disagreed on strategy … then I relieved him."

"Where is he?" asked Mori.

"He escaped not long ago. I don't know where he is."

Mori tightened her jaw before exhaling heavily. "You need to watch these people, Magakisca. This whole division is a cauldron of lost men, mercenaries, and victims out for revenge."

"I know," replied Stone. "And it's my job to make an army out of them."

Mori could see the frustration and anguish on Stone's face. She had been so busy focusing on what she had wanted him to be, she had forgotten to think about the pressures of his new position. She glanced over his shoulder toward the body of Captain Larson. "Your captain, he was a brave solider. He saved your life," she said, suddenly realizing she had almost lost him.

"I'm so sick of this killing," declared Stone. "But we must win in order to find peace in the future."

"I'm sorry for before," said Mori. "I shouldn't have questioned the abilities of your men, and I will fully support your orders."

"Thank you," replied Stone.

"And I will not press you on our future until after this mission is complete," she added, although her stomach wrenched with anxiety.

***

Captain Springfall swung his rifle toward the stairway as Captain Rain dashed to the other side of the entrance. Shifting his line of fire upward and to the right as he slowly ascended the stairs, Springfall heard footsteps on the floor above. He stopped on the landing between floors and motioned for Rain to move forward before he started up the second set of stairs. He covered the entrance to the second floor as Rain moved past him. At the top, Rain removed his hand from the handguard of his rifle and motioned for Springfall to join him.

Once on the second floor, Springfall glanced to Rain, who pointed toward the second door at the right of the hallway. Springfall saw a shadow move in the small line of light at the bottom of the door and signaled Rain to take up position to prepare to force entry into the room. In response, Rain slowly shifted to his right with his rifle at the ready.

Springfall raised his left hand, showing three fingers. Then two …

A blast from a riot gun tore through the closed door from the other side, sending Rain tumbling backwards in a hail of splinters and lead as Springfall's rifle erupted.

"Contact!" shouted Springfall into the comms circuit, stepping forward and kicking the door open.

Stepping through the entrance, he saw a man level a rifle toward him. Springfall felt the recoil of his rifle as he fired, knocking the man to the ground. Springfall spun to his right toward a wounded man on the floor behind the door. The man raised a pistol and fired as bullets from

Springfall's rifle peppered the wall and shredded the man's torso.

Springfall fell to one knee as a bullet struck his thigh. He was pushing himself to his feet when another bullet struck his shoulder, knocking him to the ground. He pulled a pistol from his vest and swung it toward the new threat, only to have it kicked free of his grip as a man standing over him crashed his boot into Springfall's hand.

Grunting, Springfall pushed himself up, but his back slammed against the floor as the man drove him downward with a foot on the Ranger's injured shoulder.

Springfall reached for the man's leg, but another round tore into his right shoulder.

"Stay down, Ranger," grumbled a tall, powerful man with a tightly trimmed beard.

Breathing heavily from a combination of pain and anger, Springfall gazed upward toward his attacker. "Do it," he grumbled.

"Don't worry, Ranger," the man replied. "I'm not going to kill you. I need you to deliver a message for me."

Springfall felt the pressure of the man's pistol against his neck as the man leaned in close to him.

"Tell your General Stone that Brand Maxa sends his regards."

Springfall shifted his head slightly, grunting as the pistol pressed harder against his neck.

"And tell him that I will have my revenge," he added, slamming the pistol against Springfall's temple, knocking him unconscious.

***

Martin walked along the firing line as her team completed their daily range training. The digital scores changed above each shooter's lane, but Martin didn't need to check the results; everyone on her team was an expert. She waited for a lull in the gunfire. "Cease fire!" she yelled, activating the hold fire siren. "Lock and clear all weapons!"

"Who has the highest score?" asked Praetorian Oxia.

"You can measure your dick against the others later, Praetorian," replied Martin.

"I'm pretty sure Graves has you beat, Sir," joked Shara.

"You're just jealous, Shara," replied Graves, raising her middle finger to the first sergeant. "Come on over and I'll show ya just how big it is … with all due respect, First Sergeant," she added.

Martin fought back a smile as she watched Oxia fume. "As much as I would like to let you guys and your little sewing circle chat, I have some word to put out. Gather 'round," she said, waving for the team to form around her. "I expect we'll be back out in the nothing in a few weeks to find the Traitor, so it's time to lay out the teams."

Sergeant Graves raised her hand as if she was a student asking a question for lecture. Martin thought this would be interesting.

"Questions already, Sergeant?" she asked.

"Yes, Ma'am," replied Graves. "Will Shara have his own team? … I'm just asking because I'm guessing it will take a whole shuttle for him, his ego, and his fat ass."

"Don't forget my porn," added Shara.

"Paladin Martin," interrupted Oxia. "Can we please get to the assignments?"

"Of course, Praetorian. We will have two teams. Alpha Team will be led by Captain Desro and consist of Lieutenant Plaxis, First Sergeant Shara, and — you're welcome Graves — Sergeant Graves."

"And Bravo Team?" asked Oxia.

"Well, that'll be everyone else," answered Martin sarcastically.

"Who will command?"

Martin let out an exasperated puff of air. "Lieutenant Messer is the senior officer on that team."

"So neither of the First Family officers are in a command position?" asked Oxia.

Martin saw everyone turn toward Oxia. "This is effectively an Elite Guard unit, Praetorian … and as such, seniority and combat records dictate who commands, not family status."

"Is that really common practice —"

"If you don't like your assignment, Praetorian, you can always go back to babysitting the ProConsul."

The Praetorian stood silent.

"Good," continued Martin. "We'll start going over possible locations to pick up his trail tomorrow, and I'll expect each team leader to prepare tactical and environmental briefs based on the planets we may be visiting two standard days later." Martin looked over the group. "Dismissed."

The group began to disperse and gather up their gear.

"Captain Desro, Lieutenant Plaxis, and First Sergeant, I need you three to stick around … more admin crap with your transfers from your units."

"Do you need me?" asked Lieutenant Messer.

"Your paperwork came through this morning," replied Martin. "You're off the hook."

"Aye, Major," replied Messer. "I'll see you tomorrow," he added with a salute before joining the others leaving.

"I'm guessing this isn't about paperwork," asked Shara.

"No," replied Martin. "We need to talk about how we are going to deal with the others."

"We might as well start with the privileged elephant in the room … Oxia," said Desro.

"How the hell did he get on this team anyway?" asked Shara.

"Courtesy of the ProConsul," replied Martin. "He's our official babysitter."

"Well that's gonna be a problem for us, Ma'am," said Shara.

"But one we're stuck with," said Martin. "We just need to watch what we say around him, and if possible keep him on the team that will be chasing dead ends."

"So that's the reason for two teams."

"Partially. I needed time to get this thing growing," she said, raising her new hand slightly, "so I had to pick a number for the team that would take a while to reach."

"So what about the others?" asked Desro.

"I don't know enough about Messer," said Martin. "But he volunteered, and I couldn't turn him down with his record ... Varus would find out and ask questions."

"He's a good officer," replied Desro. "But I don't know his politics."

"You said we could count on Graves?" said Martin to Shara.

"We can. I'm just waiting for the word."

"The Marine will take some talking, but he'll do the right thing," said Martin. "But we need to wait until we are in the Dark Zone to tell them ... I don't want to take any risks in case we are wrong."

"And if they don't go along?" asked Desro.

"Then we deal with them," said Martin, contemplating the possibility of tangling with both Graves and Mack if they didn't go along with the plan.

"So what's our first move?" continued Desro.

"The decoy team will head to Port Royal. It will get them out of the way while not raising any questions with the ProConsul," replied Martin.

"And us?" asked Plaxis.

"We're going to meet Stone."

"Where?" asked Shara.

"I'm keeping that right here," she answered, pressing her finger against her head, "until our first jump."

"Then what?"

"We stay out for a bit, make some periodic reports, and when it's close to the party starting, we jump back to our side so I can reassure those involved and get ready to make mischief when the shooting starts." Martin noticed a troubled look on Plaxis's face. "What is it?"

"How are we going to deal with the pilot and navigator of our transport?" he asked.

"I'll be our pilot and navigator," replied Martin.

"You can fly a transport?" asked Plaxis.

"She can definitely crash one; I can testify to that," laughed Shara.

"Let's hope our future landings are much less exciting than that one," said Martin.

"And our support units?" asked Desro.

"Won't have any," answered Martin. "Another benefit of a bigger team: no one should question not having a support unit. And if they do, I'll just say they would slow us down."

"Any more info on the objectives of this … revolt … revolution … whatever?" asked Shara.

"Not sharing that information yet, First Sergeant. If no one knows all the details, it's less likely it will be compromised."

"Wonderful," replied Shara. "Kept in the dark … just like the rest of my career."

"Then you should be used to it, First Sergeant," said Martin. "Now, if that's it, we should call it a night."

Plaxis and Shara began to move toward the exit.

Martin noticed Desro hadn't moved.

"What is it, Venny?"

"You better be right on this one, Emily."

"I am."

"If you're wrong or this goes sideways, we'll be lucky if they just crucify us … not to mention what they will do to our families…"

"Don't forget, Venny, our families — our entire civilization — is why we are doing this," said Martin, placing her hand on his shoulder. She winced, the new flesh on her hand still tender.

"You better get that hand healed fast," warned Desro. "I'm thinking you're gonna need 'em both soon."

***

"Next round is on the Corps," said Shara to Mack, slamming a mug of beer in front of the Marine, causing a small amount to spill onto the table.

Mack looked up disappointedly at Shara. "You can sure as hell bet a Marine wouldn't waste a drop of this fine beverage," he said with a smile.

"Fine beverage?" replied Graves. "More like lukewarm piss."

"You Guardsmen sure are picky ... didn't peg you for the champagne type, Sergeant," said Mack, mocking Graves.

Graves laughed out loud. "Champagne is for those First Family bitches and their wives," she said before putting the mug to her mouth and emptying it in a series of large gulps. "I'm more of a whiskey girl," she added, standing to get another drink from the bar.

"You keep your seat, Sergeant," said Mack, extending his hand toward Graves. "The Corps can get this one," he continued, glancing toward Shara.

"Now that's inter-service cooperation," replied Shara. He could feel his face growing warm from the three previous rounds. "I'll take —"

"The sergeant said whiskey," interrupted Mack. "So it'll be whiskey."

"I'll take a shot of whiskey," declared Shara, pretending it was his decision.

"I'll be back," said Mack as he stood and left for the bar.

"He's an odd one," remarked Shara.

"You mean he's a mature, level-headed, and professional soldier?" asked Graves, her lip curled and head tilted.

"Yeah. Exactly. I thought Marines were supposed to be just a step above a merc when they were on liberty."

"Well, we can't all be like you," said Graves with another smirk before glancing toward Mack. "Besides, I'm sure he was a handful as a corporal back in the day."

"Looking for a little 'hand-to-hand' with the Master Guns," joked Shara. As soon as he spoke, Shara winced as Graves punched his shoulder. "Damn, Sarah," he grumbled. "I was just givin' ya shit." Even a half-drunken punch from a Guardsman still hurt.

"Jackass," replied Graves. "Sometimes I wonder how you made First Sergeant."

"I'm really good at shooting things and blowing shit up," he replied with a smile.

"I got something for you to blow."

"Dirty," replied Shara. "And besides, I thought you were saving yourself for the jarhead."

He braced himself for the punch he knew was coming.

This time, Graves drove her fist into his thigh.

Caressing his thigh under the table, he conceded. "Fine. You win."

"Whatever," replied Graves, feigning anger.

Shara had known Graves for four years; he knew she liked the ribbing because it was the way the enlisted in the Guard talked to one another. When she first joined, Shara remembered a First Family lieutenant who had treated her with kid gloves … until she broke his nose in a sparring match.

And he knew she really did want the Marine. Graves wouldn't touch a fellow Guardsman and rarely found a man or woman she felt up to the task, but when she did, she went after them like a lioness goes after a gazelle. "So … I'm gonna head out after this next round and leave you two kids alone," he said.

"Do what you want," replied Graves. "Makes no matter to me."

Shara smiled.

"Shut up!" she demanded. "Just finish your drink."

"You're the boss, Sergeant," said Shara, gulping down the rest of his beer. "Happy hunting," he added as he stood from the table.

"Where are you going?" asked Mack, standing in front of Shara with three shots of whiskey in his hands.

"Sorry, Master Guns," said Shara as he took one of the glasses and threw the shot down his throat. Swallowing again as his body warmed from the whiskey, he continued. "It's past my bedtime."

He glanced toward Graves, who avoided eye contact. "I'll leave the pillaging to you two tonight."

***

"Funny," posed Mack as Shara walked away. "I heard he was a handful on liberty … seems pretty tame to me."

"Oh, he has his moments," laughed Graves.

She took the glass from Mack and dipped her finger into the whiskey. Swirling her finger slightly, she then placed it in her mouth and sucked it dry as she looked up toward Mack. "Tasty."

"I'm sure it is," replied Mack with a knowing smile.

"Wanna head out, Master Guns?" she asked.

"Lead the way," he replied. "And you can call me Stephen."

"No," she replied before throwing the shot back and slamming the glass onto the table. "I prefer Master Guns."

"And what should I call you?" asked Mack, leaning across the table toward her.

"You can call me Sergeant Graves for now," she replied, standing and tossing a credit chip onto the table. "But you can call me whatever the fuck you want to in about fifteen minutes."

"Ooh-rah," said Mack with a smile as he stood.

"Ooh-fuckin'-rah," replied Graves.

Chapter 11

"Let's hear the numbers," ordered Stone as he sat across from his commanders. He had been in command of the troops on Kilo 7 for five months, and his plan had slowly begun to win over the population and turn the tide of the war.

Colonel Scarus stood and pressed a keypad illuminating a 3-D map. "We have stopped all progress of the enemy's main military forces and have begun to push them back in sectors three and six while holding steady in five. We have also transferred several villages over to local military forces as the enemy is pushed back."

"And my brigade has begun to expand to sectors one and four, with very good results," added General Winterbird.

"Casualties?" asked Stone.

"They aren't very tactically minded, but are fearless. Between First and Third Brigades, we have sustained one hundred five casualties, including fifteen killed in the last three standard weeks, while inflicting approximately two to three thousand casualties."

"Civilian casualties?" Stone knew a lot of the fighting had ended up in the villages.

Scarus selected another button on his keypad and several lights illuminated around various villages on the map. "Several villages in the path of our main push have received moderate damage. Luckily, most were depopulated at the time of the fighting." Scarus paused. "A few were not so lucky."

"What are the numbers?" asked Stone. "Don't sugar-coat it."

"We think casualties are in the low hundreds."

"And how many have been moved into safe zones?"

"We believe close to thirty thousand."

"Our intake numbers support that, Sir," added Vae. "Last night our total register of intakes was just under twenty-nine thousand for the last three weeks."

"Internal problems?" asked Stone.

"We've had three attacks within our lines in the last three weeks. Eleven wounded and three killed. The local authorities have also captured about one hundred Followers of the Word. Our teams supported three of their raids," answered Vae.

"Special Operations?"

Still seated, Mori activated another key. Several locations on the map illuminated.

"Scout Rangers from Alpha Company have conducted ten raids internal to the safe zones on both high value and heavily armed targets. All raids were successful with two wounded. We have also responded to three boundary incidents and Bravo Company has carried out six raids in support of First Brigade offensive operation. Total casualties for Alpha are one killed and three wounded."

"And how are Captains Rain and Springfall?" asked Stone.

"They are doing well. Captain Rain has returned to duty and Springfall should very soon."

"Good to hear," replied Stone. "Any word on Maxa?"

"Nothing since the sniper attack," replied Mori. "His trail has gone dead."

Stone nodded. He had made yet another enemy in Brand Maxa, but he couldn't think about that too much now. Stone let the numbers provided by his subordinates run through his mind. Attacks inside the safe zone were down, and villagers continued to move into their perimeter for protection. The loss of several villages, and hundreds of civilians, was regrettable, but overall, it could have been much worse. His troops were moving forward, Followers of the Word were retreating, and the villages thought the safe zones were safe. "What about the other sectors?"

"Although we have little presence there," replied Winterbird, "we have been contacted by several local authorities and, as a result, have begun to provide technical and logistical support to those resisting the Word. We have also heard rumors of uprisings from within territory under control of the Followers of the Word."

"This is good news," replied Stone.

"Also, local leaders have reported that significant numbers of inhabitants have come forward and asked to volunteer to join our forces."

"Haven't the local military authorities enlisted them?"

"Well, Sir," said Vae, "they have enlisted close to seven thousand new recruits, but these want to fight with us … and not just on this planet."

"So they want to enlist in the Akota army?"

"Yes, Sir."

Stone stood silent.

"What should we do about them?" asked Winterbird.

"How many are there?"

"About three thousand."

"Son of a bitch," declared Mori from across the table.

"That many?"

"Yes, Sir," answered Winterbird.

"Detach Major Juli from Third Brigade. Have him select a company-sized unit to act as trainers for the volunteers. They will be attached to Colonel Vae for administrative purposes. Once we see how they are performing, I will notify the Akota command and request they formally be added to our unit."

"Yes, Sir," replied Winterbird.

"They have seen the way of their long-lost cousins and want to join us in the Great Circle," said Mori. "And it is due to your efforts, Magakisca."

"You keep this up, Sir," added Vae, "and our little division will end up a Corps."

"Let's not get ahead of ourselves," replied Stone. "I'm not even sure we should let them join us. Don't forget that long after we leave, the locals will still be fighting against the remnants of the Word."

"Yes, Sir," replied Vae.

"Any oh-by-the-ways?" asked Stone.

"Yes," replied Mori. "I will be transferring command to Captain Shay for the next few weeks, as I have a priority mission to complete."

"I'd like you to stay behind and discuss your assignment." Stone knew it was the long-awaited meeting with Martin which Mori was speaking of — a meeting he was supposed to attend.

Mori nodded in acknowledgment.

"Now," continued Stone as he rose to his feet, "if that's it, everyone is dismissed. Have a good evening."

As the last of the officers left the room. Mori moved toward Stone, embracing him. Even though they were in the same command, the last few months had been hectic and both of them had stayed focused on the mission. The two had rarely been alone. He had barely touched her and ached to do so.

"That feels good," he said, holding her close.

"It does," she replied, looking up toward him. "I wish I could stay here to help finish what you've started."

"One of us has to meet Martin; she won't give the information to anyone else."

"Are you sure she'll accept it if you're not there? It's not like she and I are friends."

"She will," replied Stone. "She'll have to. I can't leave my command when we are so close to something tangible here, and you are the only Akota she has met … and not killed."

"I'm not so sure that's not on her to-do list," said Mori with a smile. "She's already tried once."

"That was before —"

"Joking, Magakisca," interrupted Mori. "Just saying we're not going to be … never mind. You know what I mean."

"I do."

"Honestly, I'm glad you won't be going."

"Why?"

"I am concerned that this Red Wolf warrior has too much influence on you, Magakisca. I know she is brave and has what she believes to be noble intentions, but I am afraid she will resist you accepting your true self."

Stone stepped away slightly, still holding Mori's arms in his hands. "She only wants what is best for the Humani people."

"But what if she is wrong? She is so angry and sees only revenge. Until she moves past that, she will never see the truth."

"You must give her time, Ino'ka. She is … she …"

"I'll do my best, Magakisca. But enough about her," said Mori, running her hands over his chest. "I will be leaving soon, and we actually have a few moments together," she added, dropping her combat belt to the ground. "We should take advantage of it."

***

Martin paced back and forth at the entrance to Governor Maris Centius's main residence. Using the need to interview one of Centius's private security guards for her eam as her cover story, she had traveled halfway across Alpha Humana to meet with another name on Nero's list. She glanced toward a security guard. He stood tall and proud, glaring at her with a scowl painted on his face. Martin held her gaze for a second and then looked away with quick chuckle.

Through the ivy-covered bars of the main gate, she saw a well-dressed man approaching. He stopped at the gate, giving a slight bow.

"I am Vena Tal, the Governor's head of household affairs. Governor Centius will see you, ProConsul," said the man, nodding toward the security guard.

The gate slowly opened and Martin stepped inside.

"Follow me, Paladin," said Vena, and the two began to make their way to the large villa about a hundred meters away.

Martin's heart raced as she walked with the man; each of these meetings was just as likely to end in her death as it was with another ally.

"So you need to speak with the Governor regarding one of his security members?" asked Vena as they walked. "About what?"

"That's for the Governor and me to discuss," replied Martin.

"Of course, ProConsul," replied Vena. "I am assuming this will be a short visit. The Governor is entertaining friends, but will obviously see an envoy of the ProConsul."

"How very subservient of him," replied Martin with a smile. "And it won't be long, but I will need to speak to him in private."

"Surely you can discuss the matter with the Governor's guest … they are all First Family members of the highest standing."

"Sure," replied Martin. "Let me just contact the ProConsul and let her know the Governor's butler thinks he is better at determining matters of intelligence security than she is."

Vena nodded his head in acknowledgment. "I am sure the Governor won't mind stepping away from his company," he said, stopping before two massive, wooden doors. "After you, ProConsul."

Martin stepped into spacious room, decorated with antique furniture and artifacts. The villa was much more opulent than others she had seen — almost rivaling the Varus estate.

"This way to the dining hall," said Vena with a wave of his hand.

Martin followed Vena through the large receiving room and down a short hallway. Near the end of the hallway, the sound of voices and light string music could be heard. She took a deep breath as she turned the corner.

A large table came into view. At the table sat Governor Centius and his wife, as well as two other First Family members Martin did not recognize. The Governor was graying and slightly overweight, but his body still showed signs of an active lifestyle, including several years in the Humani military.

"Ah, Paladin Martin," declared Centius, looking up from the table. "I am told the ProConsul has sent you to take my best guard."

"The ProConsul has sent me," replied Martin. "But I must talk to you privately regarding the details, Governor … ProConsul's orders."

The Governor let out a chuckle. "Well, we must not go against the ProConsul's wishes."

"No," replied Martin, not sure if he was being sarcastic.

She stood motionless for a moment.

"Alright then, Paladin," said Centius, rising from his chair. "Two of my guests have yet to arrive, so the meal has not been presented yet.

Please follow me to my study, Paladin," he said, his eyes betraying a hint of nervousness.

"Very well, Governor," replied Martin. "We should —"

"Presenting Marack and Mrs. Vanara," announced Vena, interrupting Martin.

Martin's heart stopped. It couldn't be them. Not now. Not here.

She spun around to see her mother, Nia, and the man she had left both her and her father for so many years ago.

Their eyes met and Nia froze in her tracks, gripping Marack's arm tightly.

"Paladin," said Centius. "Is everything okay?"

Martin couldn't move or talk. She hadn't seen the woman who had brought so much pain into her life for almost two decades, and now she was standing in front of her. All of those years of pain and anger exploded from someplace deep within her, but she couldn't react.

"Hello, Emily," said Nia.

The sound of her voice brought her back to when she was a teenager. Her body grew hot as if her skin would catch fire. Martin instinctively stepped toward Nia, causing her mother to step backwards.

Martin stopped. She noticed her breath was heavy as she stared at Nia, still unable to speak.

"You know each other?" asked Centius.

The two women locked their gaze on one another.

"Lady Vanara?" asked Centius.

"We —"

"No," replied Martin, interrupting Nia. "I do not know this …" Rage coursed through her veins, screaming for her to choke the life out of Nia. "… woman."

"We were not aware that Paladin Martin would be here," added Marack Vanara, placing a hand on Nia's arm to calm her. "Perhaps we should reschedule our —"

"That won't be necessary," said Martin through her teeth. "My business here is done."

"But we have not yet discussed your reason for —"

"I don't want your guard," interrupted Martin, her gaze still locked on her mother.

"But you —"

"I said I don't want him," barked Martin, turning her head toward Centius.

"Very well then, Paladin," replied Centius, brushing off her gruff response. "As you are a representative of the ProConsul, would you like to join us for dinner before you leave?"

Martin could tell in Centius's eyes that he wanted to talk to her. Maybe he knew about the plot already. Either way, it was too late. There was no way she could discuss the plot with anyone that friendly with the Vanara family, or her manipulative and opportunistic mother. Even if Centius was just socializing, Martin couldn't take the chance.

"No thank you, Governor," she replied, turning back to Nia and Marack. "I seem to have lost my appetite."

"As you wish," said Centius. "I will have Vena show you the way out."

"I can find my own way out, Governor," replied Martin. "Thank you for your time."

Martin exited the room, walking past Nia and Marack. As she neared her mother, Nia slowly extended her arm to touch Martin's. Seeing Nia's hand, Martin quickly spun to one side to avoid her mother's touch. She stopped, her body tense with anger as she stared into Nia's eyes. So many things flashed through her mind.

She wanted to tell her mother how much she had hurt her. That she had broken her father. That every part of her being wanted to beat the life out of her.

But she said nothing. She wouldn't give her the satisfaction of showing her just how much pain she had caused. With an exhale, Martin turned and walked away.

Martin made her way out of the villa and across the property to the ivy gate. At the gate she stopped and turned toward the guard.

The guard stared blankly at Martin.

"Open it," she said.

"I haven't received authoriz —"

Martin cut the guard short as she slammed him against the wall of his post shack. Pinning the man against the wall with one hand, she reached past him and activated the gate.

"Thanks," she said as she stepped away from the guard and through the gate.

Once on the other side of the gate, she picked up her pace as she headed back toward her shuttle. With each step, the pain she had repressed in the villa grew stronger until she stopped, unable to catch her breath. Stepping off the walkway and leaning against the back of one of the large trees lining the way, she began to take deep breaths as the frustration and pain she had held back in the villa poured out of her.

Tears rolled down her face, and she let out heavy puffs of air as she relived the day her mother walked out on her family. She let herself remember the first time she saw her father passed out drunk, and recalled that day in the market with Marack's asshole nephew. Turning, she slammed her fist into the tree, forgetting how sensitive it was.

Pain shot through her body like a bolt of lightning and she fell to the ground, letting out a groan of agony. Leaning against the tree, she grabbed her new hand with the other and breathed through the pain as she let the pain in her arm replace the pain in her heart. After a few moments, she pulled herself to her feet.

"Fuck her," she said, dusting off her uniform.

***

"A Mr. Artemis to see the ProConsul," said a Praetorian standing near Astra Varus's chair.

"Let him in," replied Astra.

The doors to Astra's chambers slowly opened, and Artemis walked inside.

"Good evening, ProConsul," said Artemis as he strode across the room.

"Halt!" ordered the Praetorian, stepping in front of Artemis. "The ProConsul has not given permission to approach."

Artemis stopped. A smile came to his face as he looked around the Praetorian toward Astra.

"He may approach, Praetorian," said Astra. "And you may take your leave."

"Yes, ProConsul," replied the Praetorian before exiting the chamber.

"Your watchdogs are very protective, ProConsul," said Artemis.

"They would not be good watchdogs otherwise, Mr. Artemis."

"I find loyalty to be a little too … predicable."

"And that is why I pay you what I do, Mr. Artemis."

"And that's why you get information like I have for you today, ProConsul."

"Well then, what do you have for me? Start with Martin."

"I haven't found anything to report, but I would caution you, ProConsul. Her hatred for the First Families and for you specifically is evident … but I don't think this is news to you."

"She is a loud, arrogant, disrespectful piece of street trash … but she is also deadly, and I think she may hate Stone more than she hates me. These loyal-to-the-end types take betrayal hard, and Stone being painted as a traitor crushed her. She will have no other focus until he is dead." Astra paused. "And she is one of those rare breeds of killer who thinks every violent, rage-filled atrocity she commits is part of some grand gesture of service to her people." A smile came to Astra's face. "Don't worry, Mr. Artemis. I will never trust her. And I have put measures in place beyond hiring you to keep an eye on her …

but I will definitely use her until she is no longer needed."

"Then I guess you will be more interested in the other information I have?"

"The Dorans? Yes, tell me what you have for me."

"The agents I placed in the recreation houses have begun to send in reports."

Astra leaned forward from her chair. Hopefully she would finally gain the edge over her Doran watchdogs. "Go on, Mr. Artemis."

"I have full reports here," continued Artemis, handing a data chip to Astra.

Astra took the chip in her hands. "What are the highlights?"

"The Dorans don't seem to have any plans that directly involve Alpha Humana other than that they were directed by the Xen Emperor to support you."

Astra let out a quick sigh of relief. At least they weren't after her directly. "What else have you learned?"

"The Dorans are having internal political problems."

"Interesting," replied Astra.

"It appears there is a power struggle between the two Doran Kings involving settlement of new planets."

"And how does this affect Zorlar?"

"His cousin, King Vali, readily agreed to provide this force in hopes of gaining Xen favor

in the dispute. It appears the other King, King
Bal, died about one standard year ago, and after a
small power struggle, his eldest son, Ja-li, came to
power. Vali had supported the other son, which
caused bad blood between the two lines. Once in
power, Ja-li authorized settlement of a planet that
had been nominally assigned to the Southern
multi-polis — Vali's people. Vali protested, but
Ja-li still allowed the first settlers to land. Now
Vali has sent his own settlers to a nearby location.
It is apparently a tense situation, but Vali has
appealed to the Xen for arbitration. This
expeditionary group is a show of his loyalty to the
Xen Emperor."

"With the Dorans still in open conflict with
one of the Terillian tribes, the threat of civil war
must be very taxing on their leadership," mused
Astra. "Zorlar's performance could directly
impact the Xen decision to support his King's
claim on the settlement issue."

"That about sums it up, ProConsul."

"So it holds true that, once again, there's no
better way to get information from a man than
though his penis."

"Money's not the only thing that makes the
worlds go 'round, ProConsul," replied Artemis
with a smile.

"Does that mean you're asking for a bonus,
Mr. Artemis?" asked Astra, running her hand
down her cheek as she leaned forward from her
throne.

"From what I've heard, that would be quite a bonus, ProConsul … and most likely my downfall."

"Afraid of flying too close to a star, Mr. Artemis?" she said, rising from her chair and walking toward Artemis.

"Not at all, ProConsul," replied Artemis. "Just trying to get the lay of the land."

"You think too much, my clever little spy," she said, running her hand over his cheek.

He grabbed her, pulling her close. "You can't think too much when power, money, or sex is involved, ProConsul."

Astra let out a light gasp but let him press his body against hers. She wasn't sure if she was doing this to make sure she had control of him or just because she needed the release.

"If you have to think about sex," whispered Astra, "you're doing it wrong."

Astra felt a bolt of excitement shoot through her as Artemis slid his hand down her side onto her rear, squeezing tightly.

"So, ProConsul, which is it? Are you trying to seduce me to make sure you have control of me … or do you just need a good rogering?"

Astra let out a moan as Artemis grabbed her hair and pulled it tightly.

"Either way, Mr. Artemis," replied Astra, gripping Artemis's crouch. "You've given me information I can use and now I am offering you something you'll never forget."

She stepped away from Artemis and began walking toward the private exit leading to her personal chambers. A few meters from the door she stopped, turning back toward Artemis. "Are you coming, Mr. Artemis?"

Astra turned and continued to walk away, a smile coming to her face at the sound of Artemis's footsteps walking her way.

Chapter 12

Senator Luecentius Malius glanced to his right, then to his left. The chaotic noise of the Mt. Castra market place sounded like drums pounding inside his head but was nothing compared to the beating of his heart. Covered by a hooded cloak, he quickly made his way through the textile venders. Everywhere he looked, it seemed there was a constable or a military guard. Since the enactment of martial law, the subtle elements of control of the Humani civilization had become overt, day-to-day manifestations of the ProConsul's power.

"For your lady," shouted an adolescent boy, shoving a roll of cloth in Malius's face.

Malius stepped away from vendor, turning his head.

"C'mon mister," pleaded the boy, tugging at Malius's cloak.

Malius gripped the cloak tightly, holding it
over his head as he rushed away from the boy.
"Let me be," he grunted.

Pushing his way through the crowd, Malius
threw himself against the wall at the edge of the
market. Breathing heavily, he looked across the
frothing sea of humanity in front of him.
Scanning to his left, he saw it. A small red circle
with a line through it painted on a building a few
meters away. Pulling his cloak even tighter,
Malius took a deep breath and pushed his way
toward the mark.

Reaching the building, Malius turned quickly
down a tight alley. The smell of smoke, aging
meat, and urine burned his nostrils. Trying to
keep his head down, Malius crashed into
something and fell to ground.

"Watch where you're going!" shouted a large
man as Malius felt himself jerked to his feet and
slammed against the wall of the alley.

Malius looked into the dark eyes of a large,
bearded man. The smell of alcohol permeated the
air around him as he spoke.

"Aren't you a fancy —"

***

Martin drove her boot into the back of the
knee of the man pinning the Senator against the
wall, sending him to ground. Martin pivoted and
sent another boot to the side of his head,
knocking him unconscious.

"Don't hurt me!" pleaded Malius, cowering against the wall.

"Damn it, Senator," cursed Martin. "It's me. And what part of 'don't draw attention to yourself' didn't you understand?"

"Paladin Martin," said Malius with a sigh of relief.

"Just shut up and follow me," she said as she pulled Malius back to his feet.

Martin mumbled curses about First Family members to herself for the next few meters until she reached a small door.

"In here," she said, opening the door.

Malius stopped at the door, looking back toward Martin.

"Just go, Senator. Nothing in there's gonna bite you," she said, giving Malius a gentle shove into the room.

"Malius?" declared General Darius Vanari as the Senator and Martin entered the dusty, dimly-lit room.

"General Vanari?" replied Malius. "I had no idea you were — Senator Tyris, you as well."

"I don't think you three need to introduce yourselves," said Martin. "You all know why you are here."

The three First Family members — two Senators and a general — sat in near darkness waiting for Emily Martin to speak.

"Are we the only ones?" asked General Vanari.

Even in the dimly lit room, Martin could see the anxiety on his face.

"No," she replied, "but you're not going to know who the others are."

"You're asking us to risk everything, but you're not even willing to tell us who else is involved?" huffed Malius.

"Sure, Senator," replied Martin. "I'll tell you the names of everyone involved."

"Good," said Malius.

"And then I'll tell everyone else your name. How does that sound? That way if any one of you are caught or decide to talk to Astra Varus, she can have everyone's name." Martin paused to let her words sink in with the three. "Do you want the names?"

"That will not be necessary, Paladin," replied Tyris.

"Good. This is what you will need to know. Sometime in the next six standard months, a Terillian fleet will attack Alpha Humana."

"What?" shouted General Vanari, rising to his feet. "I did not sign up be an ally of the Ters."

Martin drew her sidearm and Vanari froze.

"First, General," said Martin. "The fleet will be carrying an army led by former Humani soldiers. And their goal won't be to conquer, but to support our revolution."

"Nero's men?" asked Vanari.

"Yes."

"And how are you sure that is their goal?" asked Tyris. "How can you be sure it isn't some lie?"

"Lie?" growled Martin. "Are you fucking kidding me? You are still reaping the benefits of a lie that has made us slaves of the Xen for generations, and you have the audacity to ask if this is a lie?" She stepped toward Tyris. The Senator took a step backwards, bumping against the wall behind him.

"If it was up to me, I'd put a bullet in each of your brains and be done with it," she paused, still holding her pistol in her hand. "But Nero and Stone say they need you," she added, sliding her pistol into its holster. "So I guess I'll just have to let you live."

From the look on the men's faces, she'd made her point. "When the attack comes, General Vanari, you will order your troops to Vae and wait for further orders. Senator Malius, you will join General Vanari and prepare to act as the senior political representative in the Vae region."

"What about my own territory?" asked Vanari.

Martin let out an audible groan. "We are doing this for the entire planet … and your actions will be vital to the successful revolt. You must do this."

Vanari nodded in agreement. "I will do my part."

"And my role?" asked Tyris.

"You will need to stay in the capital and provide intelligence once the attack begins. I will provide you with a secure communications device once we are closer to the attack."

"And until then we do what? Just sit on our asses?" asked Vanari.

"I'm pretty sure that's how you spend most of your time already," replied Martin. "Just keep your mouths shut and wait for the signal, and do your part."

"What happens if this doesn't work?" asked Malius.

"We all die … hopefully before we are crucified," replied Martin. "And some of us will probably die even if this plan works."

"You are asking a lot, Paladin," replied Malius.

"I'm asking you to do something for your people for once in your fucking lives," shot back Martin. She paused, wondering if talking to them had been a mistake. "And don't forget, you're already in this by showing up," she added. "So if any of you are thinking about turning on the others, I can promise you that unlike Astra Varus, I will kill you quickly … but not too quickly."

"We are with you," said Tyris.

"Good," said Martin, moving toward the door. "Wait a few minutes, and then leave one at a time."

Martin watched as Malius and Vanari exited one at time. After a few minutes, she turned toward Senator Tyris. "It's your turn."

"You will have to forgive us, Paladin," said the Senator. "This is all very new to us. We are risking everything we know for this," he added. "And regardless of how little you think of us, we do want to end Astra Varus's rule."

"You do realize the goal is to bring all of it down," said Martin. "Not just the ProConsul, but the system that holds people down based simply on their last names."

"I understand," replied Tyris. "But you must understand this is not easy for us."

"It won't be easy for any of us, Senator. Revolutions aren't supposed to be easy."

"What do we do if this does work?" he asked.

"You lead," said Martin. "And not for yourselves, but for your people."

"We will do our best," replied Tyris. "But we are almost as afraid of our people as we are of Astra Varus and the Xen."

"Well, that's your own fault," said Martin, opening the door. "You should go."

With a nod, Tyris stepped into the alley.

As Tyris exited, Martin sat on the bench in the dark room. She had no idea how Stone or Nero had any faith in these men. She had met with three other small groups, and every one of these meetings caused her to hate the First

Families a little more — even the ones trying to overthrow Astra Varus.

"Assholes," she said aloud, rising to her feet and opening the door to the marketplace.

Entering the main marketplace, she saw flashing sign above a rickety door: FREE DRINKS FOR ALL UNIFORMED PATRIOTS. She looked into the window to see a smoke-filled room with a full stock of alcohol on the far wall.

"Fuck it," she said aloud as she opened the door to the bar.

***

Martin slowly opened her eyes. Her scarlet hair fell over the side of her face as she lay on a rough bed, allowing only small rays of light through. She brushed her hair aside, immediately closing her eyes as the early morning light felt like needles. She suddenly noticed her mouth was dry and chalky. Rolling onto her back, she looked up toward the ceiling of the room as her head began to pound with each beating of her heart. Her elbow pumped against something and she turned to see the naked torso of a large, muscled man in his forties lying next to her.

"Shit," she mouthed, her body aching and the memory of the previous night flashing into her conscious. She looked toward the man again, this time lifting the blanket and looking at the rest of his body. "Hmm," she huffed before the contents of her stomach began to churn.

Kicking her feet off the side of the bed and leaning forward, she took in three heavy breaths. Tightening her throat to keep from vomiting, she looked to the table on the right and saw three empty bottles. Behind the bottles, she saw the military cap of a Master Sergeant. "Damn it," she said, slowly forcing air from her body.

The warmth of a hand on her naked hip told her he was awake.

"Good morning, sweetheart," said the man.

Martin pushed her hair over her head and took another deep breath. She didn't lose control this way often, but when she did, she went all out.

"Good morning," she replied, forcing a smile to her face and turning toward the man.

Again she took in his body … there was definitely a reason she must have picked him other than the alcohol. He may have been in his forties, but had the body of a twenty-five year old-guardsman. The only man she knew that looked that good for his age was — "Damn it," she said aloud.

"What's wrong, honey?" asked the man, running his hand up her thigh.

"Nothing," she snapped, jumping out of the bed and attempting to cover herself with a pillow.

"Why so jumpy?" asked man. "You weren't so shy last night."

"Yeah," she said with a smile. "About that."

"You were incredible," he said. "I mean I've never had —"

"Thanks," interrupted Martin. "I'd had a lot to drink last night and just … let's just … I need to go?"

"So soon," pouted the man. "Are you sure you don't need one more for the road?"

"Thanks. And it was nice, but I really have to go."

"Sure, honey. Do you need money for transportation back —"

"No," blurted Martin. She paused. Maybe he didn't know who she was. It would be so much better that way. "But thanks; I just gotta get ready for my shift at the base."

"I didn't realize Paladins moonlighted," said the man, smiling.

"Oh … you know …" She wished she could just melt into the floor. "Look, can we just keep this between us, uh …"

"Taylor's my name."

"Of course it is," she replied. "But I just really need —"

"Don't worry, Ma'am," replied Taylor, holding his hand up to show a wedding ring. "I'm not gonna tell anyone."

"Thanks," she replied, hating herself even more now. "I'm just gonna grab my things and be on my way."

Martin quickly stepped into her pants and threw her undershirt on. *I'll never do this again,* she thought to herself, but at the same time knew she probably would.

"You really were incredible," said Taylor, still lying naked in the bed.

"Thanks," she replied, buttoning her shirt.

"If you ever need to, uh —"

"I think I'll pass, Taylor," said Martin, sliding on her boots, "I don't think your wife would approve."

"Probably not," replied Taylor. "But I'm willing to take the chance."

Now her stomach churned from Taylor's words as much as her hangover.

"I'm good," she said, quickly making her way to the door of the recreation room.

Stepping outside, she leaned against the wall and looked up toward the ceiling. Despite her splitting headache, she began to pound her head against the wall. "Stupid, stupid, stupid," she said aloud. She looked down at her feet before taking another deep breath and scurrying toward the exit of the recreation house.

Chapter 13

General Stone and his brigade commanders sat in a large meeting hall with the civilian and military leaders of Kilo 7 as they discussed the transition of power to local authorities. It had taken almost six months, but he was prepared to hand over control of the planet back to its inhabitants. And not a moment too soon; his division needed to prepare for the attack on Alpha Humana, now only three months away.

"Shall we begin, General?" asked Council Leader Braydon, head of the Kilo 7's civilian leadership.

"First we will start with the transition of key cities. General Vae?" asked Stone.

"Things are going well, Sir," replied Vae, now elevated to the rank of general. "Local forces have taken control of all cities with the exception of Inotib, where the transition is scheduled to be complete in three standard days."

A tall man in a local military uniform stood to speak. "General Vae's assistance has been very much appreciated. My security forces are currently performing concurrent patrols with General Vae's troops, and will undergo communications and tactical response evaluations tomorrow that will be the final step in completing the transition."

"Excellent, General Jollie. General Winterbird, what is your status?"

"My troops have overseen the beginning of repopulation of villages and have completed basic training of volunteer units to provide security during the transition. Our logistics support has been established to provide equipment requests through Akota command as necessary. We have also completed the basic training of twenty-five hundred volunteers for our division in the last three months. They will require more specialized training, but they are prepared to join the command."

"Our Council has sent a representative to your Akota leadership to help coordinate this support," added a graying man in civilian clothing.

"I have received word from the Shirt-Wearers that Ambassador Page has safely arrived and should be establishing communications through normal and secure methods within the next standard week."

Stone turned toward General Scarus. "What is the status of our offensive operations?"

"The addition of General Vae's forces have allowed us, with the support of growing local military and civilian support, to defeat the last standing army the Word had in the field. There are still several pockets of resistance, but from a military standpoint, they are well within the means of local forces."

Another officer from Kilo 7 rose to speak. "We still expect sporadic violence and will be prepared to provide a measured response if necessary."

"But will this be enough?" asked another civilian.

"It's not a great answer, Representative Tara, but you won't know until it happens," replied Stone. "As I have said many times, your planet has been infected with this religious movement, not unlike a body is infected with a disease. We've stopped the symptoms and hopefully prevented it from spreading and causing more damage, but you'll probably never really be cured of it. You're going to need to work at it every day."

"And you think we are now prepared to do this?" asked Tara. "What if we are not?"

"If you are not, then we will return."

"And don't forget, Representative Tara," added General Jollie, "they will be leaving a regiment behind to assist in further training and to provide support if necessary."

"Will that be enough?" asked another representative.

"You must take this next step yourselves, gentlemen," replied Stone. "If you want this planet to truly belong to your people again, you do not want us to occupy Kilo 7 indefinitely. We will help if needed, but you have to lead the way."

"We understand, General," replied Council Leader Braydon. "But you must understand the concerns of many … we were so very close to losing everything."

"Then remember how close you were to the brink and work every day toward preventing that from happening again," replied Stone.

"Of course, General," replied Braydon. "I think if the representatives have no further questions, we should let our subordinates get back to completing the transition."

"I concur, Council Leader."

"Very well, then," said Braydon. "If there are no more questions or motions, then this meeting of the Council is concluded."

After a few moments of speaking with the Kilo 7 leaders, Stone walked with General Vae as they left the meeting hall.

"Do you think they will succeed here, General?" asked Vae.

"Hell, General," said Stone, "I don't even know if we were successful. I just know it's better than it was."

"So you think we may be back here someday?"

"I hope not, but I would never say never, General Vae. But for now we have our next assignment. It's time to return to Akota territory and prepare for the attack on Alpha Humana."

***

"That's the last of the gear, Major," said First Sergeant Shara.

"Good," replied Martin. "Everyone gather up!"

Sergeant Graves and Captain Desro joined Shara and Martin at the access to their transport.

"We'll head out in one hour. Bravo Team will depart in two days for —" She paused. "Where's Plaxis?"

"I thought he was with you, Major?" answered Desro. "I —"

"Plaxis has been assigned to Bravo by order of the ProConsul," interrupted Lieutenant Oxia as he walked out of the transport.

"What the hell are you talking about, Praetorian?" demanded Martin.

Oxia stepped in front of the group. "The ProConsul has taken great interest in your mission and decided she would rather have me assigned to the team you were leading."

"I don't fucking think so, Praetorian. The ProConsul doesn't choose how I assign my teams."

"I believe the ProConsul does as she pleases, Paladin Martin," replied Oxia.

"Captain Desro, find Lieutenant Plaxis and tell him to get his ass on this transport in fifteen minutes."

"Yes, Maj —"

"Lieutenant Plaxis has been ordered to General Vispa's headquarters regarding First Family security risks," replied Oxia. "In other words, none of your concern."

"Everyone take five!" ordered Martin, her gaze locked on Oxia.

"Roger that," replied Shara, already walking away.

With a glance to see the others walking away, Martin quickly looked back toward Oxia. "I don't know what the fuck you are trying to pull here, Oxia, but it ain't gonna fly."

"I am only doing as I am ordered, Paladin Martin," answered Oxia with a smile. "The ProConsul ordered me to see her last night and gave me my orders." He extended a handwritten order with the ProConsul and Varus family crest at the top. "Even though I think you are little more than a low-class assassin, I agreed to follow your orders … as long as they did not contradict the ProConsul's. And this letter trumps your wishes, Paladin."

Martin felt as if her skin would catch fire as she quietly read the order. Was Astra onto her or the plot? Or was she just being cautious? Or just a bitch? "I need to contact the ProConsul."

"I am sorry," replied Oxia, "but she informed me … well, ordered me to tell you she would be on Lord General Zorlar's flagship most of the day and directed me to — and I am quoting her — 'tell Paladin Martin she needs to remember her place.'"

She couldn't challenge a direct order from the ProConsul; that would draw too much attention — and possibly confirm Astra's fears of a plot, if she had any. "Fine, Praetorian. You're on my fucking team," she conceded with scowl. "But the only thing the ProConsul has ordered me to do is to take you with me. Beyond that, you fucking Praetorian robot, you will follow every fucking order I give or I'll knock that privileged smirk off your face."

"Of course, Paladin Martin," replied Oxia. "I," he added as he looked directly into Martin's eyes, "don't need to be told to follow orders."

"Just get on the fucking transport, Lieutenant."

"Yes, Ma'am," replied Oxia with a salute.

Martin looked down at the orders in her hand, crumbling the paper into a tight ball. "Everybody load up!" she shouted so that the others could hear.

Shara and Graves were the first to reach the transport.

"So what's up, Major?" asked Shara.

"Looks like we're taking the Praetorian instead of Plaxis."

"No difference to me, one First Family officer for another," said Graves. "Just point me toward the enemy, Major. That's all I give a shit about."

"He's going with us?" asked Shara, his concern showing.

"Is that a problem for you, First Sergeant?" replied Martin.

"Not a problem, Major," answered Shara, shrugging his shoulders. "Should've known better than to try to understand why you officers do anything the way you do."

"That's what happens when you think too hard, First Sergeant," said Martin. "Now load up."

"Yes, Ma'am," he replied, giving Martin a quick glance of confusion as he walked up the ramp to the transport.

Martin gave him a nod to acknowledge she knew things just got bad.

"So what happened, Emily?" asked Desro, now standing next to her.

"Son of bitch got Astra Varus to order that he follow me … or Astra Varus ordered him on her own."

"Do you think she knows about the plot?"

"I don't think so … if she did, we would already be dead or on our way to Capro." She stopped, her brow furrowed. "Or she is using us as bait to draw out other supporters or to find Stone."

"You said this plan would work, Emily," said Desro, glancing toward the transport. "If that son of a bitch is a spy?"

"Oh, he's a fucking spy, Venny. I just don't know if he knows anything or not."

"Well if he doesn't know, he's gonna know soon enough when we show up for a meeting with the Terillians and General Stone."

"You don't think I know that? Just … I'll deal with it. I just need some time to figure it out."

"Well, you've got about a week and a half, Emily."

"Thanks. Maybe I'll just shoot him in the back of the head and dump him out of the garbage shoot," replied Martin as she started up the ramp.

"Funny."

"I'm not kidding," she said, turning back toward Desro. "But for now, I just want to get this can out of orbit."

Martin walked into the troop compartment where Shara and Graves were sitting, through the small passageway with the access to the engine room on each side, and into the flight control compartment leading to the cockpit. Once there, she checked the engineering status panel to verify controls were set to automatic and ran the hull containment check protocols. Satisfied, she moved forward toward the cockpit. Opening the door, she saw Lieutenant Oxia standing between the pilot and navigator seats.

"Where are the pilot and navigator?" he asked.

"You're looking at them," replied Martin.

"You?"

"You signed yourself up for this mission, Praetorian. If you don't like it … I'll open the fucking door for you right now."

"This is highly irregular, not having a pilot or navigator."

"This entire mission is irregular … and in case you have forgotten, highly classified. If I fly and handle the navigational plots, that's two less people that have to be debriefed."

"And what if you become incapacitated?"

"Then I guess you better figure out how to fly a transport, Praetorian," she replied, brushing past Oxia and sitting in the pilot seat.

"And where are we going?"

"You'll find out when the rest of the team does."

"And why do we have to wait? Bravo Team has known they are going to Port Royal for a week."

"Everyone knows we will be looking at Port Royal, so it made no difference. Our destination is need to know," said Martin, running the Master Systems Alarm and Warning check sequence.

"I have the highest level of classification, Paladin. I am a Praetorian Officer and —"

Martin turned and rose from the pilot seat as the alarms began blaring and the systems test ran their course. "And I determine what you need to know and when you need to know it, Lieutenant. I have actually spilled, and shed, blood with other members of this team, and they don't know, either. Do you see them asking me where we are going?"

"They are not my concern. I —"

"Everyone on this fucking ship is your concern, you son of a bitch," she exploded, shoving Oxia backwards.

Oxia stumbled but regained his footing. Anger washed over his face as he gripped his sword. "You can't —"

Before his could start to unsheathe his sword, Martin's was at her side.

"You're not guarding the damn ProConsul anymore, Praetorian. Out there in the nothing, you will be expected to watch our backs, and we will watch yours ... that's what soldiers do."

"Are you challenging me?" asked Oxia, slowly pulling his sword from its sheath.

"If it's a fight you want, Praetorian, I'll give you one. But I think the ProConsul would rather we find the Traitor than have your body delivered to her after I open up your chest."

Oxia paused. "You are right, Paladin. The mission must come first; but be assured, the ProConsul will hear of all of this when we return."

"I'm sure she will, Praetorian," she replied sheathing her sword. "Now, if you don't mind, I need to get this ship in the air."

Martin returned to the pilot seat and acknowledged that the alarm and warning checks were complete.

"Fine," said Oxia. "But I still want —"

"I'm doing mission stuff, Praetorian. Go away. You're bothering me."

Martin watched Oxia fume in the reflection of the airflow status screen on her control panel. After a few seconds, the Praetorian officer turned and stormed out of the cockpit.

"Damn it," she said aloud, smacking her fist against the control panel. Maybe she should've just killed him then. There was no way the situation wouldn't come to a head in the next few days, and he would have to be handled. But she also needed a story that Astra would believe, and she was pretty sure Astra Varus was close to reaching her fill of tall tales from her.

"I'll think about that tomorrow," she said as she began the reactor startup sequence.

***

Astra slowly rose from her knees. Her skin was warm and clammy, dotted with beads of sweat from the heat and humidity of the room.

She hated reporting to the reptilian Xen ambassadors, and the fact that the environments of their estates were unfit for any respecting Humani made it that much worse. Mimicking the Xen home planet environment, their homes and offices remained at a steady ninety-five degrees fahrenheit and near one hundred percent humidity.

"We are pleased to see you," hissed the Xennite advisor, Dlackar.

"I, ProConsul Varus, leader of the Humani people, am honored to have the privilege to serve the Empire and the Emperor," she responded, wiping sweat from her brow.

"As am I, Lord General Zorlar, Head of the Yellow River Clan, Cousin to King Vali of the Doran Southern Multi-polis, and combined leader of the Doran Humani Expeditionary Group."

"What information do you have for us?" added Vartor, the other advisor.

Astra glanced toward Zorlar from the corner of her eye, sweat rolling down her face.

"Wise and clever advisors," added Astra, "the flow of slaves from Bravo system has not only reached the requested numbers, but has increased to make up for previous shortcomings." She turned slightly, smiling toward Zorlar and then toward the advisors. "None of which would have been available without the support and guidance of Lord

General Zorlar. His leadership and support of the Empire has resulted in the Senate awarding him our highest honor, and because of his efforts, I humbly request his name and that of his cousin, King Vali, be mentioned at the Weekly Reading to the Emperor."

Out of the corner of her eye, she saw Zorlar turn toward her. Astra knew the mentioning of his, and more importantly his family's, name at the weekly update of Empire operations to the Emperor would be a political laurel that could be used against King Vali's political opponents. And now, coming from a non-Doran, would not seem like a political move.

"This is good news, ProConsul," replied Vartor.

"And we are pleased to see our allies are cooperating as well as you are," added Dlackar. "It appears you are working well together to meet the desires of the Emperor."

"Our duty is to serve the Empire," said Zorlar, with a thankful nod toward Astra.

"And your service will be read to the Emperor," said Dlackar.

Zorlar bowed slightly. "I am honored."

"If there is no more to report," replied Vartor, "you may be excused."

Astra and Zorlar bowed in unison and turned to exit the sweltering room.

Once outside, Zorlar turned toward Astra.

"I am in your debt, ProConsul," said Zorlar.

"I spoke the truth, Lord General," replied Astra with a smile. "Your assistance has been vital to our success." Now time to reel him in. "And from what I have heard from the Advisors, your Northern King has taken too much of the spotlight from the hard work the Southern warriors have done both here and against the Terillians in your sector."

Astra saw what she could only interpret as surprise on Zorlar's face.

"We have been …" Zorlar paused. "King Vali will be informed of your support, ProConsul."

Astra smiled and nodded. Artemis had earned his pay. Zorlar had let his harsh, superior demeanor drop, if only for a moment. Favorable words on his behalf would also gain favor with his cousin, with the King, and with the Emperor. And as far as Zorlar knew, Astra had gotten the information from the Xen. "Thank you, Lord Zorlar. We are allies and therefore must look out for one another. Don't you agree?"

"Of course, ProConsul."

Chapter 14

The "thump-thump" of the music blasting inside the bar pulsed against Martin's body and reverberated in her ears as she stared at the entrance. Her heart pounded even faster than the music booming from the club. She knew she would have deal with Oxia soon, but that wasn't the cause of her apprehension. It had been a long time since the plot had been hatched … since she had seen Stone. She feared he would lose himself to the Akota ways — to that Akota woman. Which Tyler Stone would be inside the bar? The leader who had mentored her, or someone else?

"Is this shit-hole the place?" huffed Oxia.

"That's why we're fucking here," replied Martin without looking toward the Praetorian.

"Is the little bar too scary for you?" prodded Sergeant Graves. "You afraid you'll get your nails mussed up?"

Oxia turned toward Graves. "No, but I don't make a habit of wallowing in filth."

"Afraid you'll catch some disease in there?" she replied.

"I will need a shower after just stepping into this dump," replied Oxia, his nose wrinkled and mouth curled in disgust.

"You'll probably have to 'get in' a little more past the door to catch a disease, but I'm sure you can find one or two recreation girls that are all loaded up with a virus or two," said Graves with a smile.

"You can wait outside if you like," said Martin, seeing an opportunity. "In fact, you just volunteered to be the lookout."

"Do you want me to stay outside?"

"I need someone to, Lieutenant. And that someone is you."

"I don't know —"

Martin stepped in close to Oxia, looking up toward the tall, proud puppet of Astra Varus. "Are you going to follow my order or not?"

"Fine, Paladin," he conceded. "I'd rather stand in this dirty street than go into that cesspool."

"Great, can we go now?" grumbled Desro.

"Enough," interrupted Martin. She didn't want Oxia growing suspicious, and she was tired of the banter. "Fuck it," she declared as she stepped forward and pushed the door open to the ringing of bell attached to the door.

The acrid smell of incense, the flashing of strobe lights, and the roar of the music filled her senses as she stepped through the entrance. She scanned the room for Stone as the others entered behind her. "Shara, you cover the left. Graves … to the right," she ordered.

"What the hell are we looking for?" asked Graves.

"I'll tell you when I see it," replied Martin.

Martin paused as she saw Mori emerge from the mass of people in the bar. She was alone and in full uniform.

So much for subtle.

The bell at the entrance rang, and Martin turned to see Oxia enter. Her heart stopped. This was going to be bad. She quickly turned toward Oxia, her hand sliding to her pistol. "I thought I fucking told you to stay outside."

"I saw a Ter patrol and wanted to —"

"So you made it," shouted Mori over the roar of the club.

Martin saw Oxia's eyes open wide as he saw Mori. "Scout Ranger!" he shouted, reaching for his weapon.

Mori's expression tightened as she reached for her pistol.

Martin didn't have time to think; she reacted. Yanking her pistol from its holster, she placed it to Oxia's temple and fired.

The crack of Martin's pistol drowned out the music as Oxia's head jerked to the right. The crowded bar erupting into chaos as the Praetorian's body crumpled toward the floor.

"Stop!" shouted Martin as she saw Graves bring her rifle to her shoulder. "Don't shoot!"

Shara stepped in front of Graves's line of fire. Graves shifted to her right, but Shara moved to block her line of fire again.

"Get out of the fucking way!" she shouted.

"Just wait," pleaded Shara.

"What the fuck just happened?" demanded Graves, stepping backwards, her weapon shifting back and forth from Mori to Martin. "You fucking shot him!"

"What the hell is going on?" asked Mori, her weapon pointed toward Graves.

"Everybody lower your fucking weapons!" shouted Martin over the still-pounding music.

Martin looked toward Graves. Her eyes screamed, her face contorted, and her mouth was moving, but no words came out. Martin let out a grunt, raised her pistol, and fired two rounds into the sound system behind the bar of the club. "Now can we all stop fucking yelling," she said, turning back toward Graves.

"What the fuck is going on … you know this fucking Ter?"

"Lower your weapon," said Martin calmly.

Graves refused, her weapon still directed at Mori.

"Sergeant Graves, lower your weapon," repeated Martin. "That's an order."

Graves looked toward Martin, her body tense. "But —"

"Sarah," added Shara. "It's okay … just lower it."

"Somebody needs to tell me what just happened," demanded Mori, her pistol still held on Graves.

"Just a minute, damn it," replied Martin, sliding her pistol into its holster and holding her hands out to her sides in a calming gesture. "I'll explain everything — to everyone — as soon as everyone calms down!"

Mori slowly lowered her pistol and Graves followed suit as the last of the patrons scurried out of the bar.

"Paladin Martin," said Graves, "what is this about? How do you know this Ter?"

"That's Terillian, Hanmani," replied Mori. "Who are these people?" she continued, turning her gaze toward Martin.

"My team," replied Martin. "And why the fuck are you in uniform? You might as well have rung a fucking bell."

"You're within Akota lines, sweetheart," replied Mori. "Why wouldn't I wear my uniform? And it looks like being on your team is a bit dangerous," said Mori, glancing at Oxia's body.

"He … isn't on the team anymore."

"Someone tell me what the fuck is going on!" interrupted Graves.

Martin walked over to Graves and placed her hand on the barrel of her rifle. "Remember when I told you that you would learn things that would shake your beliefs? Remember when I asked if you trusted me?"

"Yes ... but —"

"Do you still trust me?"

"Yes. I just don't ... why did you kill the Praetorian?"

Martin placed her other hand on Graves's shoulder. "Everything you have heard about Stone is a lie."

"What are you talking about?"

"In fact, everything you've been told about our people ... our history — all of it — has been a lie."

"What?"

"The Xen are not our allies. They've been our masters since they invaded our planet generations ago. The First Families have ensured that their wishes have been carried out ever since. Including starting the wars against the Terillians."

Graves stumbled away from Martin's grip. "No," she gasped. "Why would you say that?"

"It's true, Sarah," added Shara.

Desro nodded, confirming Martin's words.

"No. It can't be," replied Graves, gripping her rifle tightly.

"You better get your dogs under control," said Mori, holding her pistol at her side.

"Damn it!" shouted Martin. "Everyone stand-the-fuck-down!" She turned toward Shara and Graves. "Shara, explain everything to Graves." Martin stepped toward Graves. "Sergeant, what Shara is going to say is going to be hard to believe, but it is the truth. Don't think about what you have been told your whole life … think about what you know about Shara and me." She paused. "And Stone."

Graves returned Martin's gaze. "I …"

"Do you think I would ever betray our people?" asked Martin.

"No," replied Graves.

"Then listen to Shara," said Martin. "Desro, do something with the Praetorian … now, as for you," continued Martin, turning toward Mori. "We need to talk."

"That's why I've been waiting for your ass for the last three hours," said Mori, sliding her pistol into its holster.

As Shara began to explain the lie that was Alpha Humana to the dumbfounded Sergeant Graves, Martin stepped toward Mori. She stopped directly in front of her, staring into her burning green eyes. "Where's Stone?"

"He's not here."

"No shit," grumbled Martin. "Where is he?"

"Looks like that hand's healing nicely," said Mori with a smile. "When you get that occasional little twinge of pain, do you think of me?"

"Fuck you … where's he at?" Martin rested her hand on her sword. "I won't ask again."

Mori let out frustrated groan. "Major General Stone," she grumbled, "is on another mission."

"Major General?"

"Things have changed since the last time you saw him."

Martin feared Mori and her Akota mysticism had gotten to Stone. "What have you savages done to him?"

"Watch yourself, Humani," said Mori through her teeth. "And he has done this to himself … against my …" Mori paused, taking a deep breath. "He has taken command of Nero's division and is dealing with Followers of the Word in the Kilo system."

"What happened to Nero?"

"Killed by the Saint's fanatics."

"Those lunatics are making a mess of everything." Martin's gaze shifted back to the intense green eyes of her former enemy. "That's what happens when people started looking to the sky — or to some invisible spirit — to solve their problems."

Mori's face curled into a forced smile. "I guess you Humani prefer to kill for lies instead of religion."

Martin's hand tightened around her sword and her muscles tensed as she held her stare with Mori. She wanted to react violently.

But she paused. After a long breath she replied. "Can we just talk about the plan?"

"Fine," said Mori. "What do you have for me?"

"Everything's on track. Nero's intel on the First Families was right. I have contacted as many of them as I could without giving myself away." Martin released her grip on her sword. "They are in."

"Good."

"And what about the Ter … the Akota?"

"We will be ready."

"Care to share a few more details?" replied Martin. "I need to update the key players."

"And just how much do you expect me to tell you?"

"All of it. If Stone were here —"

"Well, he's not," interrupted Mori, her jaw tightened.

"Oh," replied Martin, picking up that Mori's frustration wasn't only with her. "Sounds like your plan to brainwash him isn't going to well. You can't make him something he's not … no matter how hard you try."

"What he believes and what he and I do are none of your fucking business," said Mori.

"Touchy," said Martin with a smile. "But I still need more details."

Mori stood silently, fuming.

"Look, sweetheart. You don't like me … I get it. And I sure as shit don't like you, but we're both in this together, so just fucking tell me the details."

"I'm not in the habit of just dumping intel to Humani," replied Mori. "It's —"

"I trusted you enough to let you cut my fucking hand off, bitch. I think you could show me a little now."

"Fine," huffed Mori. "The assault force for the Gateway Station is finishing training and the last units for the orbital attack of the Dolus base have been assigned and are beginning simulated attacks."

"And the Humani invasion force?"

"That has fallen to Magakisca and his staff," said Mori. "He has been heavily involved with the insurgency of the Saint's followers in the Kilo System but his last report said he would be transferring control of security to indigenous forces any day to assume command of the assault forces."

"So Stone will be part of the land assault."

"That's what the Shirt-Wearers wanted," replied Martin. "I wasn't really involved in the decision."

Martin held back the urge to take another jab at Mori and at her apparent rift with Stone. "He is the best choice."

"Of course," replied Mori dryly.

"So everything is still on schedule?"

"We are a go two standard months from now. The first jump will reach Gateway Station at 1330 hours standard."

"Good," replied Martin. "Here are the valance sequences for transmission of jump codes on the day of the attack." She watched Mori place the chip in her pocket. "It's time the Humani people learned to live for themselves, not for the Xen … or the First Families."

"What are we going to do about Oxia?" interrupted Shara. "They will ask questions."

"You mean to say your Red Wolf here did something without thinking about the consequences?" replied Mori, her gaze locked on Martin.

"Red Wolf?" asked Shara.

"These Ters like to give you names after you kill enough of them," replied Martin, giving Mori a smile.

"Akota, you Hanmani savage," replied Mori. "And you still have a dead soldier lying there to explain to your master."

Martin clinched her teeth. She didn't need Stone's Terillian lover telling her what she had to do.

"Major?" asked Shara again. "We can't return empty-handed with the ProConsul's watchdog dead."

"We'll need to make them think we had at least some success," said Martin aloud.

"I can help with that," replied Mori. "If you're willing to accept help from an Akota?"

"And how can you help?" asked Martin.

"How about my body as proof of your success?" asked Mori.

"What the hell are you talking about? Not that I haven't thought about it," said Martin with a smirk, "but I'm guessing your boyfriend wouldn't be too happy about that."

"Well it's obviously not me," replied Mori, "but Stone knew Astra Varus would at a minimum be looking for a reason to doubt you, so we received permission from the clan of a female warrior recently killed in battle to use her body in place of mine. Her appearance, given her wounds, is close enough to pass for me."

"And where is this decoy?" asked Martin, intrigued.

"Stored on my ship," answered Mori. "She and her clan have made a hard decision in allowing her body to be given over to the Humani ... it is not our way."

"It might work," said Martin. She could tell Mori was unnerved by the body of one of her own being handed over to the ProConsul. "I can't ensure what will happen when we return," she added, "but I promise your warrior will be treated with respect until them."

"Thank you," said Mori with a nod.

"Even then, the ProConsul will question if only Oxia is dead," added Martin.

"Sorry, Major," interjected Shara, "I'm not volunteering to let you shoot me."

"Funny, Shara," replied Martin. "I don't actually plan to lose anyone else. I just need the ProConsul to think Oxia wasn't the only one killed."

She looked toward each of her team.

"This is real?" asked Graves. "What you said? It's really true?"

"It's the truth," replied Martin. "All of it."

"Then I'll do it. I'll stay behind."

"She can return with my team and then join Stone's staff," added Mori.

"Are you sure, Sergeant?" asked Martin.

"Hell no, Major," replied Graves. "But I'll do it anyway. Nobody back there to miss me."

"Thank you," said Martin. "But it can't be you. The ProConsul knows Captain Desro and First Sergeant have history with me. It should be one of them," she added, looking toward Shara.

"Oh," replied Shara. "I guess that was me volunteering?"

"It was, First Sergeant."

"Just another day in the Guard," replied Shara.

"Now that we have that taken care of, do you have anything more for me?" said Mori.

"Tell General Stone that landings would be less opposed near Vae, the Tri-Cities, or any Scarus or Eastern Family lands. The Juli family will hopefully be able to establish control of the regional government, and the Plaxia family should be able to gain control of Port Plaxia, but Stone will need to take Mt. Castra by force. I will try to disrupt their defense grid and cause as much chaos in the city as possible, but he will need at least a division to take and hold it for any length of time."

"A division?" replied Mori, shaking her head. "I keep forgetting just how many of you are crammed on that planet."

"If we can take Mt. Castra and hold it long enough, we can disrupt the planetary defense response, which should give the First Families supporting the revolt time to consolidate their power. Once that is done, the word about the truth can be spread, and more people will join the revolution."

"And if they don't join?" asked Mori.

"Then we deserve to be ruled."

Chapter 15

Martin stood in front of Desro and Shara at the entrance to the transport's cargo bay.

"If she doesn't buy this, we're dead," whispered Desro.

"You're always looking at the downside, Venny," replied Martin.

"Funny. You do know —"

Desro stopped as a Praetorian stepped into the cargo bay.

"Attention!" shouted Martin as Astra Varus, General Vispa, and Artemis entered the compartment.

"So Paladin Martin," said Astra, strolling into the compartment. "Show me the whore."

"Yes, ProConsul," replied Martin. "She is stored over here."

Martin walked over to a metal container. Unlatching the cover, she swung it open to expose the body of a Terillian warrior with long, black hair. There were two obvious bullet wounds to her torso and the right side of her face was mangled.

"Hmm," said Astra. "Seems like so much a pile of flesh and bones in this metal box." She let out a satisfied titter. "And to think of the trouble this bitch caused."

"Are we sure this is the right body?" asked Artemis, looking over the body. "How many dark-haired Terillians are there? Millions?"

"It's her," replied Martin. She moved in close to Artemis. "I know since I'm the one that killed her," she smiled. After staring at Artemis for a few seconds, she turned toward Astra. "And who is this Port Royal gutter rat?"

"The name's not important, Paladin," replied Artemis.

"That's okay," said Martin with a smile, looking him over. "Now I know what you look like," she added. "In case someone needs to identify your body someday."

"That is enough posturing," said Astra, turning to Martin. "Where is Oxia's body?"

"It was destroyed, ProConsul."

"Why was it destroyed?"

"I didn't do it, ProConsul. Both Lieutenant Oxia's and Sergeant Graves's bodies were blown apart by an explosion ... this Terillian shot Oxia and when Graves attempted to pull him to safety, they were killed by a grenade. There were only pieces left." She presented a sword. "But I did want to return his sword to the Oxia family," she added, handing the sword to General Vispa.

"Unfortunate," replied Astra. "But at least he died for his people."

"That he did, ProConsul," said Martin.

"General Vispa, have this whore's body taken to the Eternal Flame, stripped naked, and crucified for all to see until there is nothing left but bones."

"Yes, ProConsul," replied Vispa.

As Martin watched the Praetorians take the body from the cargo bay, her blood boiled at the thought of the brave warrior put on display.

"Now, as for the Traitor," said Astra. "When will I be looking at his dead body?"

"Soon, ProConsul. Soon. I have sent word to my other team to have them return. I will combine the two teams and pick up his trail again. I expect them to return in the next standard month and be after him again a few weeks after that."

"Why wait, Paladin?" asked Astra.

"We lost two men taking the whore, ProConsul. I'm guessing we'll lose more taking the Traitor."

"Since you have brought me an appetizer, I guess I can wait a little while longer for the main course." Astra paused. "But do not fail me again."

***

Martin ignored the dull pain radiating through her hand as she walked with her father in the garden of the veteran's hospital. His hand holding hers was worth it.

"I know you cannot speak about your mission, Emily," said her father, "but how much longer will you be here this time?"

"Here, father," she said, feeling his body begin to shake. "Let's sit on this bench."

He started to lower himself to the bench but lost his balance, causing Martin to grab him and direct him onto the bench. "Now, come sit with your father," he huffed, patting the bench beside him. "How long will you be here?"

Martin sat next to her father. "A few weeks, father. Then back out there."

"The word is that you killed the Traitor's woman."

"Yes," she sighed. She hated lying to him.

"What is it, Em?"

"Nothing."

"You can't fool your father, Emily," he replied, putting his hand on her shoulder. "Something is eating at you."

"What makes a warrior honorable?" she asked, her eyes red and wet.

"Emily," he said, running his hand over her cheek. "If anyone should know what it is to be an honorable warrior, it's you. You are a hero of your people."

Martin guffawed. "I'm not so sure about that."

"What is it? You can tell me."

Martin looked up toward the flashes of late afternoon light dancing among the leaves of the trees above them and sighed.

"Is it classified?"

She looked into her father's eyes. "Is a warrior's duty to the people or the Senate …" she paused, shaking her head, "… or the ProConsul?"

"I don't understand? The Senate represent the people and the ProConsul guides the Senate … it is all the same. When we say either one, we speak of the Republic and the culture and society that saved us from utter destruction."

"But what if they weren't the same? What if to save one, you had to —"

Martin felt her father's hand tighten around hers.

"You shouldn't speak of such things, Emily. It could be considered treason."

"Treason against who? If I …" She paused. Every part of her being wanted to tell him the truth. She knew her eyes had to be giving her away. But she couldn't tell him; he had dedicated his entire life to serving the ProConsuls. "Never mind," she continued, shaking her head to clear her thoughts. "Sometimes I just get … tired."

As she spoke the word "tired," a flood of emotion hit her and thoughts flashed through her mind. Thoughts of Talia Vanara accosting her in the market when she was a teenager, of her arrest for breaking Talia's nose, the frozen hell of Golf 2, the dead war dog that gave its life for the coward Sequentis Varus, and the look of hatred on the young Phelian girl's face as Martin shot her exploded in her thoughts like a series of gunshots. A wet flood of tears flowed down her face as she couldn't hold back anymore. Then the image of Jackson's face staring into hers as he died on Juliet 3 caused her to let out an audible moan as she buried her face in her hands. "I'm just so tired of everything."

Sobbing into her hands, she felt the calming hand of her father on her back. As his hand made slow circles, she took in deep breaths, regaining her composure.

"Look at me, Emily."

"I can't," she wept.

His hand moved to the back of her head. "It's not like I've never seen my daughter cry, Emily," he said calmly. "Look at me."

Martin slowly raised her head, looking into her father's eyes. "I'm sorry for —"

"You have nothing to be sorry for, Emily," interrupted her father, wiping a tear from her cheek. "Shedding tears for what you have done for your people makes you no less a warrior than the blood you have shed for them."

Martin ran the cuff of her sleeve over her eyes to dry them. "I shouldn't show such weakness. It's not becoming a soldier."

"You've shown no weakness, Emily. You've shown why you fight so hard for our people. It is that passion that makes you a great warrior."

Martin wasn't sure if he truly meant what he was saying or if he was just trying to calm his crying daughter. Either way, it worked.

Catching her breath, she spoke.

"Do you really think the First Families have the best interests of the people in their hearts?"

"They must think of the entire civilization, not the individual. If we think of ourselves over our people, we weaken the Republic. The individual makes selfish, short-sighted decisions, but the First Families make the hard decisions that will ensure the survival of our people."

"What decisions are you talking about, father?" asked Martin, her heart stopping.

He looked into her eyes, not saying a word.

"What are you talking about?" she repeated. Did he know? She felt her heart now as it pounded in her chest.

"Everything … our laws, politics, representing us to the Xen … they have the experience and the intelligence to make the right decisions for all us," he replied, spouting the same rhetoric she had heard her entire life.

Maybe he didn't know. "Don't you think we can determine our own fates?"

Her father let out a laugh that quickly turned to a cough. "I'll take the order of the First Families for the chaos of the masses any day."

"You'd rather stay in a cage for fear of what freedom might bring?"

His hand tightened around hers. "Freedom is a lie anarchists tell people who are easily manipulated and unable to earn their keep," he said, his eyes focused and intense. After a few seconds, his grip loosened. "And besides, Emily, where is this cage you speak of? All the First Families have brought us is prosperity and power."

"And war," added Martin.

"The Terillians brought this war to us, Emily. You know this … what is all of this about?"

"How can you trust them after everything … after mother —"

"She wasn't from a First Family," he replied coldly. "She simply hoped to improve her standing, which is what each one of us should do … what you have done."

"She betrayed you … betrayed us. What she did —"

"Enough!" interrupted her father, his voice carrying the power it used to when he was a Praetorian. "You can't blame the First Families for my inability to keep —"

"Don't say that," interrupted Martin, her face red hot with anger. "Don't ever say that. It was her and —"

"Perhaps we should just continue our walk," offered her father. "Let's just enjoy the garden."

She gritted her teeth and inhaled deeply, calming herself. "Sure, father," she replied. "Maybe that would be best."

"Good. Then help an old soldier to his feet," he said with a smile that barely hid his frustration.

"Yes, father," she said, rising to her feet. "Let's get you moving."

***

Martin was lost in her thoughts as she made her way back to her barracks. She ran through the list of conspirators, wondering which of them would fold at the first sign of trouble. Then she flashed back to the sight of her mother and Marack Vanara at Governor Centius's home. Her head began to ache; how she yearned for the uncomplicated violence of combat.

Suddenly she stopped in her tracks.

"It's the man with no name," she said, turning to her left toward a tall, thin man leaning against the wall of a confectionary shop.

"I guess you do remember a face," replied Artemis.

"And what is the ProConsul's spy doing out here among the common folk? You wouldn't be spying on me, would you, Mr. Anonymous?"

"Now I wouldn't be a very good spy if I answered that, would I?" Artemis pushed himself off the wall. "But then again, if I was a good spy, you would never see me."

Martin stepped in close to Artemis. "You know … whoever the hell you are, I think you are a spy, but that you also want me to know it."

"And how is dear old father?" asked Artemis.

Martin slammed Artemis against the wall, her right hand involuntarily gripping her pistol in its holster. "You stay the fuck away from my father, Port Royal scum. He served his people and deserves to be left alone."

She stepped back from Artemis, her eyes fixed on his.

"Such anger from such a beautiful woman," replied Artemis with a smile. "If you ever tire of playing soldier, you must contact me." Now it was Artemis who moved close to Martin. "With your bravery and beauty, you would make a formidable spy," he said with a wry smile. "You could be plotting against someone right under their nose and they would be none the wiser."

Martin stared coldly at Artemis, but it took all of her strength to keep her emotions from boiling to the surface. She knew he was a spy, and apparently a good one, but was he just trying to get a rise out of her or did he really know something? She could only hope he didn't. "Trust me," she replied. "I'd rather deal with my enemies face to face, looking them in eyes when I kill them."

"You are a saucy one, Paladin Martin," replied Artemis, apparently unfazed by her not-so-subtle threats. "I can see why you are one of the ProConsul's favorite pets."

"We both know I'm not one of her favorites," replied Martin. "I'm useful … that's all she cares about."

"And a realist, too," said Artemis. "Whether you know it or not, you have a knack for espionage, Paladin."

"What I have a knack for," replied Martin, "is violence. So unless you want to see just how good I am at that particular skill set, stay the fuck away from me and my father."

"As you wish, Paladin," said Artemis, with a nod. "Good day," he added before strolling away, whistiling.

***

Stone sat across from the Shirt-Wearers, waiting for them to speak.

"Welcome back to Luna-tunkan, Magakisca," said Shirt-Wearer River, rising to shake Stone's hand. "You and your troops have performed well."

"The people of Kilo 7 had more to do with it than me, or even my men, uncle," replied Stone. "They have fought hard, and will need to continue to do so to keep their planet their own."

"And soon you will have the chance to fight for your planet, Magakisca," said Shirt-Wearer Wolf.

"That is why you have been called to meet with us," added River. "We have decided to elevate you to the rank of Marshall, which will be commensurate with your roll in the attack."

"Thank you, uncle, but even with our increased numbers, my command is still not much larger than a division in size."

"True," replied River, "but you have been chosen to lead the entire assault force on Alpha Humana."

"That will be close to two hundred thousand troops under your command," added Wolf.

Suddenly, the weight of all two hundred thousand pressed down on his shoulders. "Will the Akota officers follow me?"

"General Winterbird has spoken well of your performance on Kilo 7, and word of your success is known among the Akota flag officers … they know you can fight and they will follow you."

"I am honored and accept command," replied Stone.

"Excellent," said Shirt-Wearer Shadow. "Fleet Admiral Willow and your division commanders will meet with you tomorrow so that you can get an update on the training for the attack."

"Very well, uncles," said Stone. "From what I have heard, Martin has provided excellent intelligence on recommended landing areas and First Families that will support us."

"Casualties will still be heavy, Magakisca," said River.

"They will, uncle," he replied, "and even if we gain control of key cities on Alpha Humana, we will still be facing a civil war not only on our home planet, but in every system the Humani control and even within every Humani unit." He paused, trying to contemplate the cost. "It will be bloody. Bloody unlike anything the Humani have seen."

"But if you are victorious?" posed Wolf.

"Then what is left of the Humani people will face the wrath of the Doran and Xen." He rose to his feet, emotion washing over his body. "But we will do it as a free, united people facing our true enemy."

"And with your Akota brothers and sisters at your side," added Shirt-Wearer Falling-sky.

"As allies?" posed Stone. "The fate of the Humani must be determined by the Humani people, not by the Akota or the Terillian Confederation."

"Of course," replied River with a glance toward the other Shirt-Wearers. "Our culture is one of self-determination. It is —"

"This is true, uncle," interrupted Stone, uncharacteristically, "and I mean no disrespect, but you must also be willing to accept that the Humani people may not immediately consider themselves long-lost brothers of the Akota, if at all. Are the Akota prepared to deal with a Humani people that are not willing to accept Akota culture?"

"But they are Akota," replied Falling-sky.

"They were," said Stone. "Now they …" He paused, his jaw tight. "Now we are different."

"This makes sense," added River. "But hopefully someday, we can be reunited as brothers."

"And that will be a great day, uncle," said Stone. "But if we win this battle, and the Humani can win the civil war that will surely follow, they will need allies, not long-lost relatives trying to push their culture on them. They must be allowed to find themselves and choose their own path."

"We will provide them support without pressure," said River. "We all must recognize the true enemy are the Xen."

"Once the Xen are defeated," added Wolf. "Then we can deal with the future nature of our relationship with the Humani."

Stone nodded his head. "Thank you. I will speak with Admiral Willow and ensure we are ready."

"The assault is scheduled to depart for the attack in just over a month, so we will meet again in two weeks," said River. "In the meantime, report anything that will cause a delay to the assault immediately. We are getting so very close, and we can't have any problems."

"Of course, uncles," said Stone.

Chapter 16

Targus Malius threw back a drink, swallowing hard. Sitting in a private booth inside Diamonds in the Clouds, one of the many upper-class recreation houses in Mt. Castra, he nervously awaited his guest. The vibrations of the music from the main club pulsed against his body as he poured himself another drink. "Where is he?" Targus said aloud, looking at his watch. "Do you see him?" he asked one of two large bodyguards in the room with him.

The guard opened the door and peered outside. "He's coming, Sir."

In a few seconds, a thin man wearing the uniform of regional magistrate's office stepped into the room. As he did, the bodyguards stopped him.

"Why are you in uniform?" demanded Malius.

"Is this not official business?" asked the man. "I was told by one of your servants to meet you here." He looked around the room. "This is very odd, Mr. Malius."

One of the bodyguards began to frisk the man, roughly checking his pockets.

"What is the meaning of this?"

"Sorry, you can't be too careful."

"I do work for the Magistrate, Mr. Malius," replied the man.

"Your position in the government means very little nowadays, Mr. Trent."

"He is cleared," said one of the body guards.

"Come, Mr. Trent, sit," said Malius, motioning for the man to join him. "And close the door," he told the bodyguard.

The man sat next to Malius. "Why have you called me here, Sir? And why this place?"

"What I must say needs to be said away from my father and needs to go directly to Magistrate Varus."

"What is this about?"

"Treason."

The man leaned in close to Malius.

"What are you talking about?"

"Treason on a grand scale," said Malius. "Against the ProConsul and the First Families in only three days' time."

A knock on the door drew their attention.

"Who is it? Send them away," ordered Malius.

"Yes, Sir," replied the bodyguards in unison.

The bodyguard opened the door to a beautiful red-haired woman in a tight red dress. Her hair fell over the front of her shoulders and she held a platter full of drinks.

"I have a drink for Targus Malius," she said with a smile.

"Not now," he replied. "Leave us —" He paused, rising to his feet. "How do you know —"

"Wait," pleaded the woman. "I have a message for you from Magistrate Varus," she added.

Malius stood from the couch, his body almost shaking with anxiety. "How did ... step inside, quickly," ordered Malius.

The woman stepped inside the room and a bodyguard quickly shut the door.

"Check her for weapons. Quickly."

"Where am I going to hide a weapon?" asked the woman.

"Check her!"

"Fine," she replied, setting the platter on a nearby table and raising her hands in the air as the bodyguards began to check her.

"Now, tell me how —" Malius paused, tilting his head slightly in contemplation. "Don't I know you?" asked Malius.

"I doubt it," replied the woman. "I don't work here ... I'm just a messenger."

"No. I know you ..." Malius looked over the woman. Her legs were toned and powerful

and her waist firm and tight. She was beautiful …
and strong, it looked. He then focused on her red
hair as one of the bodyguards moved it up, as if
in a ponytail, to check the back of her neck.
"Paladin!" he shouted.

***

Martin drove her fist into the throat of one
of the guards and then sent an elbow crashing
into the temple of the second as she pulled a
pistol from the first guard's belt. She spun toward
the second guard, placing the barrel against his
forehead and firing. The first guard was
attempting to push himself off the floor when
Martin pinned him to the floor with her shoe, the
heel sinking into his skin. In the chaos, Mr. Trent
leapt from the couch toward the exit, but Martin
fired a round into the side of his head before
turning and firing into the guard pinned on the
floor.

"No!" shouted Malius, already backed into
the corner of the room. "You can't —"

"I just did, you son of a bitch," interrupted
Martin, walking toward Malius.

"Everyone will have heard the gunshots," he
said. "You've killed yourself."

Martin slammed Malius against the wall,
pressing the barrel of the pistol against his
forehead. "No one heard shit," she grunted.
"You can barely hear any of that chaos outside;
what makes you think they will hear anything
from the inside?" She pressed the pistol harder

against his forehead. "And I know you First Family assholes are too concerned about your privacy for there to be visual monitoring."

"Don't kill me," he groveled, "I wasn't —"

"You were, you little prick. You were going to inform fucking Sequentis Varus about the plot … have your own family killed."

"Please don't …"

"Oh, I'd kill you just for making me have to wear this fucking dress." She slammed the pistol against his temple. "But you have done so much more."

Malius turned his gaze back toward Martin. Finding resolve in his fate, he spoke.

"Why wouldn't I?"

"You'd let your family die so you can be ruled by a race of reptiles?"

"Better than the common trash that infests this planet."

Martin slammed the pistol into his temple again.

A confident smirk came to Malius's face. "You can't kill me. Not like this. I am unarmed, with you looking me in the face like you are … you would be killing me in cold blood."

Martin threw the pistol onto the floor.

A smile came to Malius's face. "I promise I —"

Malius was interrupted as Martin's hands tightened around his neck.

"You really don't know a fucking thing about me, Targus Malius," she grunted as she placed all of her strength into her grip on Malius's neck. He attempted to resist, grabbing at her arm, but Martin slammed her fist into his nose before tightening her grip again. As she felt him begin to weaken, she leaned in close to his ear and spoke softly. "I prefer to look my enemy in the face when I kill them. And as far as a weapon goes, you were ready to kill thousands, maybe millions, with your fucking mouth, so it looks to me like you're still armed."

"Please," he coughed, trying in vain to break Martin's grip.

"Let me tell you what I will think about as I take your life … many years ago, I watched a Humani war dog give its life for Sequentis Varus after he had betrayed my men … all because of a fucking chip in its head." She felt the tears begin to flow down her cheeks as she saw the terror grow in Malius's eyes as they flashed back and forth. "Unfortunately for you, I don't have a chip … just the memory of that dog dying so that traitorous, elitist cowards could live. I tell you now, Targus Malius, I would trade every fucking First Family member on this planet for that one fucking dog."

She squeezed hard around his neck, the tears flowing freely down her face. As her eyes locked onto his, she watched red veins began to materialize in the whites of his eyes. Soon his coughing and thrashing stopped and his bloodshot, graying eyes froze.

***

Stone lay awake in his stateroom onboard the Akota carrier *Winterfall*. Staring at the overhead, he tried to run through the order of battle for his invasion force and the operations orders he would need to issue soon.

He couldn't focus. Rolling to his side, he looked at Mori as she slept. Unable to help himself, he ran his hand over her raven-colored hair. She slowly opened her eyes.

"What is it?" she asked, her brilliant green eyes still cutting straight to his soul like the very first day they met.

"You know I love you, right?"

"Yes," she replied with a smile. "But it's okay for you to wait until morning to tell me."

"I'm sorry," he said, laughing slightly. "I know it's late. But in two days everything will be different. I've been lying here for hours running every scenario through my mind. And no matter the outcome, Ino'ka, I want to be with you when it is over. I want this, what we have right here. And I want you to know that regardless of whether I am Tyler Stone, Venarius Lucius Stone, Marshall Stone, or Magakisca … whatever … none of those names changes my love for you."

He felt her hand caress his cheek.

"I want this too," she replied. "One day, when this war is over. I will hold you in my arms every night. And when that time comes, no matter what has taken us to that place, you will be my Magakisca."

"But I —"

Mori silenced him with a passionate kiss.

"Know that I love you like no other, Magakisca," she said. "Our fates are intertwined. I have dreamed it and know it will come to be." The warm pressure of her hand on his chest calmed him. "But we are near battle … we should not talk of the future tonight, but only of our love."

"I would rather show you than tell you," he said, pulling her close against his body, her warmth sending sensations over his body like electric waves.

"Then show me, Magakisca," she whispered, kissing him deeply.

***

Astra Varus took a sip of her wine and dabbed the side of her mouth with her napkin. She looked across the table she was sharing with General Vispa, Senators Marcus Sarius and Julius Lucretia, and her cousin, Magistrate Sequentis Varus. Placing the napkin on the table, she spoke.

"So cousin, what news do you have for me?"

"We have heard little by way of open resistance to the limiting of Senatorial power. Senator Centius attempted to introduce a vote that would challenge your decree, but he was easily defeated. I have added an additional team to monitor his household and servants. His head of security has also been interviewed for several hours."

"And the results?" asked Sarius.

"Nothing definitive, but we have plans in place to establish a relationship between his head of security and a known associate of the Nero family we apprehended and sent to Capro. Additionally, one of his sons has a weakness for recreation girls and one of his frequent providers is working for us. With these things in place, we will have adequate leverage to silence Centius … and charge him if necessary."

"Excellent," replied Astra. "And what of my old friend, Senator Malius?"

"He has been oddly quiet, ProConsul," answered Sequentis. "Even within the Senatorial hearings, he has done little to challenge your initiatives in the last few months."

Astra leaned forward in her chair. "That relic once took an hour to discuss how the way I walk was an example of my intent to limit Senatorial power," she said. "And when I actually take steps to do it, he says nothing?"

"It is very suspicious, ProConsul," said Sequentis. "And the death of his son, Targus, is more troubling."

"Targus Malius is dead?" asked Astra, a funny sensation running down her spine. "He was Malius's eldest, no?"

"Yes, ProConsul," replied Sequentis. "And an open supporter of your initiatives."

"When did this happen?"

"His body was found this morning in a private room in a recreation house along with two of his bodyguards and one of my agents."

"Why was one of your agents speaking with him?" asked Astra, the sensation running down her spine turning to a tightening of her stomach. "And why am I hearing of this only now?"

"I received word from local authorities just before dinner, ProConsul."

"How were they killed?"

"My agent and the bodyguards were shot, and Malius was strangled."

"What has been done about this?"

"We are investigating the scene for evidence, interviewing anyone we can place at the recreation house; I have directed additional surveillance of all members of the Malius family."

"Luecentius Malius is up to something," declared Astra. "But he would not have killed his eldest son. I want his killer found." She added, "Use whatever means necessary."

"Yes, ProConsul," replied Sequentis.

"General Vispa," said Astra, "increase the security on all facilities, and increase the Force Protection status of all units on Alpha Humana."

"Yes, ProConsul. Do you think increasing security across the planet is necessary for the death of one person? We are already at high levels of readiness with martial —"

"Do it!" shouted Astra, slamming her fist into the desk. "We must get to the bottom of this."

The opening of the door to the dining chamber drew Astra's attention. "What is the meaning of this interruption?" she demanded.

The Praetorian at the door came to attention. "Mr. Artemis requests an audience. He said it was urgent."

"Let him in," replied Astra.

"Thank you, ProConsul," said Artemis, entering the room as she spoke.

"What is the meaning of this interruption, Mr. Artemis?"

"I have someone you will want to talk to," he continued, indicating a tall, rough-looking man with a full beard standing next to him.

"And who is this?" asked Astra.

"This, my dear ProConsul, is Terillian General Brand Maxa, and he has a very interesting story to tell."

Chapter 17

Martin pulled her head above the bar as she worked out alone in the base gym. With the attack set for the next day she couldn't sleep, so she did what she always did when she couldn't sleep. Her left hand still ached, but she pushed through the pain and pulled her head above the bar again.

Everything would change tomorrow. Regardless of the outcome, she would never again have to play the pet of Astra Varus. If they were successful, she would see her people freed from the unseen yoke of the Xen and justice brought to the First Families who traded an entire planet's freedom for their own security and power. If everything went as planned, Humani High Command would get the report of an approaching Terillian fleet, and when they activated the emergency defense protocols, it would trigger the other members of the resistance to action. Dropping to the ground from the pull-up bar, she took a deep breath. Her thoughts drifted back to the day she had held the blade of her sword against Sequentis Varus's neck on Golf 2.

***

"Inform Magistrate Varus that we are secure in the Malius Fortress district," ordered Assistant Regional Magistrate Flaria as he stood over the bodies of General Vanari and his staff. "Once the men are finished collecting the bodies and checking all of the data files for evidence of further resistance members, will you need any further assistance from my constables?" he asked the Praetorian Major standing next to him.

"That will not be necessary, Magistrate. General Vanari's advance forces have been intercepted and placed under the command of Colonel Vulara near the Centius Plains region. They have been directed back into their barracks. What is the status of Vanari's family?"

"His family has been detained at their villa and are being prepared for transportation to the Magistrate Regional Headquarters," replied Flaria.

The Praetorian looked down toward the body of General Vanari. "You've reaped what you've sown, traitor," he grumbled. "And the rest will soon follow you into the nothing."

***

Martin finished her pushups and rolled onto her back. Looking up toward the high ceiling of the gymnasium, she let out a heavy breath before beginning crunches. As she began pulling her torso upward repetitively, she thought about what she and her team would do when the attack started. They would first detonate a series of charges at key communications hubs and then make their way to the Forum. Once there, while posing to assist with security, they would position themselves to take out key officers. Except for Desro and her. They would attempt to make it to Astra … and kill her.

***

"You know what you need to do?" asked Desro, holding his wife's hands tightly.

"Yes, Venny," she replied, her face flushed and her eyes red from tears. "I'll leave first thing in the morning and go to my cousin's near Ragna." He felt her grip tighten as he held her hands in his. "Are you sure this is going to work? What happens if —"

"It will work, Lana. It has to. General Stone and Emily think it will work, and I believe them. But things will be crazy for a while, and I probably won't be able to contact you."

"That's nothing new," replied Lana with a smile. "I am the wife of a Guardsman."

"You are," he replied, running his hand over her hair. "Just stay at your cousin's, and when it's over —"

A binging sound interrupted Desro. Someone was at their door.

"Who is that?" asked Lana.

"I don't know," replied Desro, knowing there was nothing good on the other side of the door. He activated the video monitor. Outside stood fellow guardsman Captain Zaria. "It's Garus," he said, pulling his pistol from a belt hanging off a nearby chair.

"What are you doing?" asked Lana. "It's Garus."

"He's a First Family member," replied Desro. "And why would he be here?"

"What are you going to do?"

He could see the terror in her eyes. "Grab the bag you packed and go to the back. If you hear anything," he said, stepping toward her, taking her face in his hands and kissing her, "run."

She stared blankly at him. The door binged again.

"Lana! Do you understand?"

"Yes," she shot back, startled from her fear of Desro's voice. "Run."

He kissed her again. "I love you," he said. "Now go get your pack."

As Lana made her way to their bedroom, Desro released the safety on his pistol and walked to the door. He took a deep breath.

"Garus," he said, opening the door. "What brings you here at this hour?"

"You need to come with me, Venny. Now."

"Why?"

Garus looked down to see the sidearm in Desro's hand.

"You know why, Venny."

"I can't come with you, Garus."

"Don't do this. Think of Lana."

"I am. That's —"

Lana's scream echoed through the apartment. He turned toward the scream as Garus lunched toward him, knocking the pistol from Desro's hand.

Desro reacted quickly, landing a right hand against Garus's jaw and wrapping his arm around Garus's neck. Garus countered, and Desro arched his body as his opponent's fist slammed into his ribs. Off balance, his feet left the ground as Garus swept his feet and drove him into the floor.

Dazed, Desro saw Garus swing his pistol toward him. He grabbed Garus's gun hand and redirected the barrel from his face as Garus fired. Desro let out a grunt as the round tore into his shoulder. Over Garus's shoulder, Desro saw two Praetorians rush through the entrance.

Rising up, he drove his forehead into Garus's nose and pulled the pistol from his opponent's hand then fired a round into each Praetorian. Before he could turn the pistol on Garus, the Guardsman pushed Desro's hand above his shoulder and shifted his body, driving his knee against Desro's throat. Struggling for air, Desro looked up toward Garus.

"Why did you betray your people?" growled Garus. "You brought this on yourself."

His head forced to the left by Garus's knee, he saw the body of one of the Praetorians lying next to him.

In the Praetorian's combat vest was knife. He tried to grab the knife but couldn't reach it.

Desro let out groan of agony as Garus shoved a hand into his wounded shoulder. Distracted by the pain, Desro lost control of the pistol. Garus grabbed the pistol and swung it toward him as Desro grabbed the knife from the Praetorian's vest.

Desro felt Garus's body go limp as he drove the knife into the side of Garus's head.

He pushed Garus's body off him and picked up the pistol. "Lana!" he shouted, heading toward the back of his house.

Turning the corner, he saw a Praetorian and fired, killing him. "Lana!" he shouted again. "Where are you?"

"She's right here, traitor," came a voice from his bedroom.

Desro slowly moved across his living room, pivoting his body as he stepped into the bedroom. Lana stood in front of the bed, shaking. A Praetorian stood behind her with a pistol to her head.

"You're gonna drop your weapon, traitor. Or else —"

Lana let out a scream as the Praetorian's head snapped backwards and he crumpled to the floor.

"Come on, Lana!" shouted Desro. "We need to go."

"What's happening?" she sobbed, falling to the floor. "What —"

"They must have found out," he said, grabbing her arm and pulling her to feet. "We've got to get out of here before —"

Desro's body went limp as automatic gunfire erupted from within the bedroom. Falling to the floor, the first thing he saw was the fan above his bed slowly turning. He coughed, feeling the blood collecting in his mouth, and slowly turned his head to his left. Lying next to him was the mangled body of Lana.

Using all of his strength, he slowly reached for her hand. "I'm sorry," he grunted, his riddled body beginning to shake.

"Well, the bitch is dead," he heard at the entrance of the room and turned to see two Praetorians standing over him.

"But the traitor's still alive," said the other one, pointing toward Desro. "We'll get some coagulates into him and maybe he'll make it so he can be shipped off to Capro."

"Praetorian," mouthed Desro.

"He's trying to talk."

One of the Praetorians knelt down next to Desro.

"Watch him," warned the other.

"He's all fucked up," replied the Praetorian. "Maybe he's ready to talk."

Desro saw the Praetorian look away to answer his companion and mustered all of his strength to pull the pistol from the Praetorian's belt. He fired into the Praetorian's body and pulled him downward as he turned the pistol on the other Praetorian. His second shot sent a round through the throat of the Praetorian before he could return fire.

The Praetorian on top of him struggled to get free, but Desro fired another round into his side before dropping his pistol and wrapping both arms around his opponent as he lay on Desro's chest.

"You have died for nothing," grunted the Praetorian. "Your revolt will fail."

Desro felt a grenade on the Praetorian's vest and grabbed it. With one arm around the wounded Praetorian's neck, he extended his other arm and activated the grenade.

"For the Republic," he coughed, closing his eyes.

***

Martin focused on the rhythmic pounding of her feet on the track. She needed to get out of her head and focus on her breathing and stride. As she felt her lungs finally begin to burn, a calm came over her; the planning was done, the mission was set, and there was nothing to do now but let it happen.

***

Sergeant Graves threw back a drink as she sat in a dark, smoky bar in the heart of the marketplace. "Give me another one," she said to the bartender.

"Rough mission coming up?" asked the bartender.

"What?" she asked.

"I know you're a Guardsman," replied the bartender. "Seen you in here before in uniform. And if you don't mind me saying, you're drinking like someone getting ready for a tough mission."

"You have no idea," said Graves with a laugh.

"Well, here's to a successful mission," said the bartender, pouring a drink for himself and holding it in the air. "This round's on me."

"Thanks."

"For the Republic," said the bartender.

"For the fucking Republic," said Graves as she finished the drink in one swallow.

Graves slammed the glass onto the bar. As she did, she noticed a hand next to the glass and felt a presence over her shoulder. She turned to see a Praetorian officer and three constables.

"Sergeant Graves?" asked the Praetorian.

"Yeah," she replied. "What do you want?"

"I've been directed to bring you to the local Magistrate's office."

"I don't think it's illegal to drink, Sir."

"This isn't a request, Sergeant. You need to come with me."

"Fine, Lieutenant," she replied. "But make it quick, I've got shit to do tomorrow."

"It will be quick, Sergeant. I'm sure of it."

Graves and the others exited the bar and began to make their way through the marketplace. Graves kept compliant but wary as she walked with the men. Eventually they turned down an abandoned street full of trash and debris. Graves noticed two of the constables slow their pace, falling behind her.

"Guessin' this is a shortcut," said Graves.

"Just follow me," replied the Praetorian.

She glanced toward one of the constables and saw his hand resting on his sidearm.

"I think I need to stop for a minute," she said.

The Praetorian stopped and turned toward her, his hand on the handle of his sword. She heard the unmistakable sound of a pistol being pulled from a holster behind her.

She raised her hands. "Hey, hold on. What's this —"

Graves dropped low and swung her legs behind her, knocking one of the constables off his feet. Rolling forward and springing to her feet, she delivered a punch to the jaw of the second constable behind her then slid behind him and drew the pistol from his holster.

The third constable opened fire, and Graves felt the rounds impacting the body of the constable she was using to shield herself as she returned fire, killing the constable. A burning sensation raced through her leg as the remaining constable opened fire. Graves pivoted and fired two rounds into the last constable's chest.

Graves stumbled, feeling a blow to her stomach followed by pressure. She looked away from the last constable to see the Praetorian's face as he drove his sword through her human shield and into her abdomen. "Son of a —" She raised her pistol and fired point-blank into his face.

Stumbling backwards, she looked down toward her stomach. "Fucking Praetorian," she cursed, pulling up her shirt to examine the wound. The blade hadn't punctured too deep but it was bleeding heavily. She turned toward the dead Praetorian. "Always fucking underestimating —"

Graves felt a sharp pain in the small of her back as a bullet tore into her spine.

Crumpling to the ground, she tried to move but couldn't. "Damn it," she groaned, unable to move her legs. She could feel the warmth of the blood on her back as it pooled under her body. Looking toward the location of the shot, she saw a tall, thin figure emerge from the shadows.

"Who are you?" she huffed, starting to feel light-headed.

"I'm someone who doesn't underestimate a Guardsman, even though you're a woman."

"Fuck off," she cursed.

"No need for bravado," replied the man. "You're gonna die. How you die depends on you."

"I'll never talk," she replied. "You can torture me all you want."

"I already said I wouldn't underestimate you, Guardsman. I know you're not going to talk," said the man as he knelt next to her. "But that won't stop them from trying."

"Well," replied Graves laughing weakly. "You broke my spine, so they only have half as many ways to hurt me."

"Unfortunately, my brave warrior, that will be more than enough."

"I still won't talk," she said. "They'll be wasting their time."

"I know."

"Who are you?"

"The name's Artemis," he replied as he pressed his pistol to Graves's temple and fired.

***

Martin slowed her pace to a walk, placing her hands on top of her head. Her heart pounded as she sucked in a few deep breaths. Slowly walking the track, she noticed the gymnastics room to her right. A smile came to her face as she left the track and walked to the room.

She walked beside the balance beam, running her hand across it as she went. She closed her eyes, remembering her days a gymnast before Nia took her father's pride and warfare took her innocence. Glancing around to ensure no one was watching, she kicked off her shoes and jumped onto the beam, pushing herself to her feet. Feeling the beam with her toes, she raised her hands into the air, cocking her head back. Leaning forward, she gripped the beam with her hands and twisted her torso, bringing her body into a perfect handstand. Turning again and shifting her weight to her right hand, she rolled back to her feet, standing.

Again she closed her eyes; she could almost hear the cheering crowd. For a moment, it all faded away. She took a deep breath and exploded forward in a series of cartwheels and flips. At the end of the beam she leapt into the air, twisting her body into two tight spirals before her feet hit the ground.

Martin took in a deep, relaxing breath. She was ready for what tomorrow would bring.

Chapter 18

Martin leaned against the wall of the elevator, lost in her thoughts. Tomorrow would be the dawn of a new era for her people and a day of reckoning for her enemies — if the plan worked.

The *bing* of the elevator told Martin she had reached her floor.

She instinctively placed her hand on her sword as the doors opened to a group of men waiting on the other side.

"Captain Cresius," said Martin, acknowledging the officer among the men.

Behind Cresius stood three other Praetorians, fully armed.

"Good evening, Paladin Martin," replied Cresius as he and the others saluted. "The ProConsul requests your presence immediately."

Martin returned the salute. "It's late, Praetorian," she replied. "Is it urgent?"

Martin saw a slight twitch of Cresius's lip.

"I am afraid it is, Paladin," he replied. "We were sent to get you immediately."

"What's with the backup dancers, Cresius?" quipped Martin as she cast a mocking look toward the guards behind him. "And they've brought all their toys."

Martin saw Cresius's completion grow red and sweat begin to form on his forehead.

"ProConsul orders, Paladin," he responded. "She has some …" he paused again.

Martin knew something was wrong.

"… some security concerns she needs to discuss with you."

"Fine," replied Martin, feigning her typical irritation with orders from Astra Varus. "Tell her highness I will be there as soon as I change," she added as she stepped past Cresius toward her quarters.

"Stop!" ordered one of the guards sternly as Martin felt another grasp her arm.

Martin turned back toward Cresius.

"You might want to teach your minions some damn respect," warned Martin.

"You need to come with us now," replied Cresius.

Martin turned her head toward the guard holding her arm. She looked directly into his eyes and smiled.

"You are about to make the worst and last mistake of your life, Praetorian," she warned.

She saw the blind pride and self-righteousness in the Praetorian's eyes. "Shut up, traitor," he ordered.

They knew.

Still returning the guard's glare, she spoke again.

"Cresius … last warning. Walk away. You don't want to die for a lie."

Cresius returned Martin's gaze. "Take h —"

Before Cresius could finish his order. Martin struck.

She grasped the arm of the guard holding her, twisting it violently outward and upward. As the guard let out scream, Martin stepped in close and landed a powerful left hand directly on the man's nose. She gripped his head by the hair and threw him to the ground, her sword flashing in the light as she pulled it from its sheath. She spun to her left, deflecting a pistol pointed toward her head by another guard, and drove her sword through his throat to the hilt.

She lost her balance as the third Praetorian slammed into her, lifting her into the air with his arms locked around her torso.

Falling, Martin wrapped her right arm around the guard's neck. She grunted loudly as her back made contact with the floor, but kept her arm locked around her opponent. Quickly wrapping her legs around the man's waist, she reached for the pistol she knew was still in the guard's holster. Grasping the weapon, she withdrew it and turned toward Cresius, who was preparing to drive his sword into her. A round from the pistol disintegrated Cresius's knee, bringing him to the ground.

Martin then twisted her body to the right and toward the first guard. He had just regained his footing when she sent a round into his shoulder, knocking him to the floor again.

On her back — her hold on the guard above her still locked in — Martin turned back toward Cresius. He had pulled himself to his hands and one good knee.

"Pssst," sounded Martin, looking down the sights of the pistol at his head.

Cresius looked up toward her.

"Warned ya," she said as she pulled the trigger and sent him toppling over with a bullet through his forehead.

"Off!" shouted Martin, shoving the pistol against the ribs of the man on top of her and firing two rounds into his torso. The body went limp on top of her and she pushed the corpse onto the floor.

Jumping to her feet, Martin scanned the area. She saw the final wounded guard scramble to his feet and rush down the passageway.

"Where are you going?" she shouted as she sprinted after him.

In an instant she was on him.

"Stop!" she ordered, sending a round past his head.

The man stopped and slowly turned around to face her. Martin could see his left arm dangling limply from the damage to his shoulder and elbow.

"I won't beg," declared the proud Praetorian.

"I won't beg," mocked Martin. "But you'll run," she added. "Such a brave little Praetorian.

"Screw you, traitor," he spat.

"That's such a funny word … traitor," answered Martin. "Against whom? Against the Humani people? The precious First Families? The Xen? The Senate? Fucking Astra Varus? Seems like traitor is a tricky word nowadays."

"You're a crazy bitch," said the guard.

"Bitch … definitely. Crazy … maybe," she said, tilting her head slightly. "But this crazy bitch can promise you that you're not leaving this hallway alive."

"Then shoot me," dared the guard. "Bring the final shame to your family … just like your whore of a mother who left you and your alcoholic father who disgraced our order."

A shot echoed through the passageway and the Praetorian fell to the floor.

"Fuck," she cursed as she paced in a small circle, trying to calm herself and contemplate her next move. Was it just her they were after or was her whole team in danger? "Damn it." Either way, she had to act. She walked back to the elevator, her body still radiating rage from the words of the Praetorian.

Entering the vestibule, she saw Cresius and another guard sprawled on the floor, blood pooling around their bodies. The third guard was also dead but had fallen to his knees with Martin's blade still embedded in his neck. She took a deep breath, gripped her sword, and quickly pulled it from the man's corpse.

She had to warn the others, if they were still alive. Her sword in one hand, she grabbed a rifle from one of the fallen Praetorians with the other and rushed toward her quarters where she could prepare herself and contact the others … and the Akota fleet that was about to appear in Humani territory. With a quick glance toward the carnage she had left behind, she rushed toward her quarters.

A few meters from her room, she came to an abrupt stop.

That same gut feeling that had kept her alive on countless missions sent warning signals rushing through her body. She slowly moved to her door and, taking cover against the wall, activated the hatch. The door slid open followed by a barrage of gunfire.

Martin spun away from the opening and curled her body against the wall as dozens of rounds slammed into the wall opposite the door. From her protected position, she pulled the grenade she had taken from one of the dead

Praetorians from her pocket, activated it, and tossed it into her quarters.

"Grenade!" she heard someone shout from the room as a Praetorian bolted through the doors.

Martin was ready and sent a volley tearing through his body just as the grenade detonated and the man evaporated in a wave of fire. The blast magnified by the confined space, Martin felt the heat and pressure against her body as the energy focused though the open door. Quickly recovering, she entered her quarters.

Dust and debris floated to the floor of the smoke-filled apartment. Looking down the barrel of the rifle as she scanned the room, she saw a Praetorian rise from the rubble that used to be a bar. She felt the recoil of her rifle and saw the man disappear from her sights. Looking around the room, she saw the bodies of two more Praetorians among the wreckage.

And the remnants of a smoldering communications station.

"Son of bitch!" cursed Martin, throwing her rifle to the ground. She would have to find another way to warn the others.

Stepping over the rubble in her path, Martin moved to the door of her bedroom and kicked it open with an angry grunt. The room was unaffected by the explosion and Martin headed directly to her weapons safe.

She punched in the combination — her commissioning date — and the door slid open to display an assortment of weapons and gear.

Martin quickly grabbed a tactical vest already prepared with two knives, handgun ammo, Humani exchange cards, and a medical kit on the back. She drew her sword from its sheath on her belt and slid it into the one attached to the back of her vest.

Next she dropped her belt and grabbed another with an additional knife, more ammo, and a pistol at each side. After affixing the belt to her waist and clamping both holsters to her thighs, she grabbed several clips of rifle ammunition and stuffed her cargo pockets.

Martin then grabbed for an assault rifle but stopped. At the top of her weapons case was a row of photos. There was one of her at her commissioning with Stone and Jackson. Another of Jackson and her at their wedding. She exhaled a heavy, pained breath when she saw the last picture. A photo of her when she was six, held by her father in his full-dress Praetorian uniform.

"I hope you'll understand it's for the good of the people," she spoke to her father's image as she pulled the rifle from its latch, shoved a magazine into it, and depressed the charging button to send a round into the chamber.

She turned away from the safe and let out another long breath before stepping into the wrecked main room.

Martin saw movement as she entered the room and instantly brought her rifle to her shoulder. Looking down the barrel she saw a young, frail Mt. Castra constable holding a pistol. His eyes were opened wide and his gun-hand was shaking.

"St-Stop right there!" he shouted, placing a second hand on his pistol in an attempt to steady his aim.

Martin lowered her rifle.

"You're Paladin Martin," he stated.

"I am. Now let me pass," she warned.

"I-I can't. They passed on the comms circuits that you are wanted for treason," he replied in a voice almost as shaky as his hands.

The constable jumped and fired a round several feet from Martin's head as she brought her rifle to the ready at her waist.

Martin jerked slightly and closed her eyes for a moment before opening them. She stared into the eyes of the skittish constable.

"Kid," she warned as she let her rifle drop to her side, suspended by the sling attached to her vest. She slowly drew her sword. "You realize you're screwing with the top of the food chain here. I don't have time for this, so move aside or I will gut you where you stand and leave you to die alone holding your own insides," she added, walking toward the constable.

The shaking had expanded from the constable's hands to his entire body as he lowered his weapon and held his head toward the floor, refusing to look into her eyes.

"Good choice," said Martin, taking the pistol from his hands and throwing it across the room. "I'll need this too," she added as she pulled the portable civil security comms radio from his vest.

The constable kept his gaze locked on the debris-covered floor.

"Who else are they going after?" asked Martin.

"The rest of your team."

"Shit. Who else?"

"A bunch of First Family members, ten or twelve I think. And a bunch of their supporters."

"What are the names?"

"I don't know?"

Martin kicked the back of the constable's leg and drove him to his knees. Gripping his hair, she placed her sword against his neck.

"Tell me the names," she demanded. The smell of ammonia in the air told her he had wet himself.

"I don't know!" he sobbed. "Civil Security was just assigned to block off key routes and pick up secondary suspects. I wasn't even supposed to be here … I heard the gunfire and came to investigate while I was going to meet up the team apprehending your father."

Martin slammed the man onto his back by his hair and pressed down hard on his chest with her boot.

"My father?" she asked in a calm tone that still betrayed a torrent of rage and violence that lay just below.

"I'm just following orders," pleaded the man.

Martin placed the tip of her sword on the constable's chest and slowly pushed the blade slightly into his flesh. "The day has come when that's no longer an excuse ... for any of us."

"Please," he begged. "Don't kill me."

"My father ...?"

"We were supposed to take him into custody and bring him to the Praetorians at the ProConsul's estate."

"Fucking Astra Varus!" she exclaimed as she crashed her boot into the constable's temple, knocking him unconscious.

Martin quickly slid her sword back into its sheath and dug in the constable's pockets for the keycard to his patrol shuttle. Two thoughts consumed her — saving her father and then unleashing years of pent-up wrath on Astra Varus.

Placing the keys in her pocket, Martin raced out of her quarters and took a sharp right toward the stairway. She moved quickly down each floor until she burst through the door on the ground level. Martin held her rifle to her shoulder as she quickly scanned the area for any threats and for the constable's shuttle. Moving around the corner of the building, Martin saw the constable's car. She quickly checked her flanks for Praetorians or other constables and sprinted across the small grass area to the car.

She jumped into the shuttle and inserted the keycard to activate the thrusters and electronic equipment. Her heart raced and tears flowed freely at the thought of her father in Capro prison. She pressed the controls of the shuttle and it lunged forward then quickly accelerated.

As she sped toward her father, Martin listened to the chatter over the Civil Security frequency.

Everything was coming undone. The constables had been placed under direct control of the Praetorians by order of the ProConsul and were setting up checkpoints throughout Mt. Castra. The same was happening in other cities throughout Alpha Humana. She slammed her fist against the dash in frustration. "Come on!" she shouted over the radio chatter, trying to will the shuttle car, already at top speed, to move faster.

Before long, she saw the retirement facility come into view. Her focus centered on the front door to the facility where three patrol shuttles were parked immediately in front of the entrance. She saw a door open on one of the shuttles and a constable step out, fully armed. Her vision tunneled as she bore down on the constable.

The man looked toward the approaching shuttle. Assuming it was another of his companions, he raised his hand.

Martin continued at full speed. She saw the constable's expression turn to surprise as she drove straight for him. He tried to swing his rifle toward her but it was too late. As he opened fire, Martin slammed her shuttle into the parked vehicle, crushing the man in a twisted wreck of metal.

Shaking off the impact, Martin grabbed her rifle and jumped from the wrecked patrol shuttle.

The constable was still alive, his screams reverberating against the nearby buildings. Martin ignored him and rushed toward the entrance of the retirement facility. As she neared the door, two more constables rushed out to investigate the sound of the crash and gunfire.

"Hal —"

The constable's order was cut short by another blast from Martin's rifle, he and the other man tumbling backwards onto the ground.

Martin continued moving forward.

One of the constables was still alive and reached for his pistol. Martin fired a round into the man's forehead as she rushed past him and burst into the main lobby of the facility.

She scanned the room while orderlies and nurses scattered and dove for cover. Moving past the front desk, she turned down the hallway toward her father's room. She sensed movement behind her and turned to see a large orderly rushing toward her with a metal object in his hand. A single round to his leg dropped him to the floor and she turned back to the hallway.

Martin carefully scanned the onrush of terrified patients and employees as she looked for threats. A frightened nurse stumbled and fell in front of her. Without looking at her, Martin grabbed the nurse with her left hand.

"Get out of the way!" she grumbled, yanking the trembling nurse behind her.

As she made her last turn, Martin saw a constable step out of her father's room. She pulled the trigger, and the impact lifted the constable into the air and twisted him back into the room.

Her heart raced as she rushed to the door and pivoted into the room, rifle at the ready.

On the floor lay a constable with her father's Praetorian sword embedded in his chest.

"Father!" she shouted frantically. "Father!"

She heard a groan to her right and spun to see her father lying on the floor beside his overturned leather chair. Her rifle hit the floor as she rushed to father's side.

Kneeling beside him, Martin looked for injuries. His chest and stomach were bleeding from several wounds.

"It's okay. It's okay," she mumbled as she tried to apply pressure to the wounds, but there were too many … blood seeped everywhere. "It's okay," she said again, reaching for the medical pack on her vest.

"Stop," replied her father in a weak voice as he grasped for her hand.

"I can fix this," she pleaded, tears clouding her vision.

"Stop!" he replied, mustering enough strength to speak in that booming, powerful tone she had known as a child.

The volume of his voice startled Martin, and she dropped the neuro-med she had in her hand.

"But —"

"It's okay," he interrupted as the volume of his voice quickly trailed off to barely more than a whisper. "Don't waste that on me. You'll need it."

"I'm sorry I didn't get to you on time," she sobbed.

She felt his hand weakly grip her forearm.

"This is a good day for me," he said in a weak, raspy voice. "I will die with the smell of gunpowder in the air, blood flowing from my body, and my blade in my enemy." Despite his weakening voice, his eyes burned bright with the fury of warrior.

Martin knew her father; this is how he would want to die. And the way she would want to, as well.

"They came to arrest you for what I have done," said Martin. "No matter what you heard from them —"

"I know ..." He coughed. "... Everything."

"What?" exhaled a dumbfounded Martin.

"The Xen and the First Families ... the secret of the war," he continued.

"But —" He had known the whole time? Martin's head raced and she felt sick. Then the truth she had been subconsciously avoiding hit her like a brick — he was the head of the ProConsul's personal guard; how could he not know?

"I am sorry for deceiving you." His voiced was now a whisper, forcing her to lean in close to him. "And I was too weak, no, too frightened to do anything about it. So I served, like I always had, and hoped that service would be enough. But when the constables came ..." Another violent cough shook his entire body. "... And they said you had committed treason, I knew you were doing what I could not. You can right my wrongs, your family's wrongs ... everything."

Martin could not find the words.

"Don't hate me for my weakness," he mouthed as his hand released hers and fell to the floor.

She stared into the face of the man she had lived her life to please as he breathed his last breath. In his final words, he had both confessed his greatest sin and laid the freedom of her entire people on her shoulders.

"I'll make it right," she whispered into his ear as her tears fell upon his cheek.

"Don't move!" boomed a voice from behind her.

Martin raised slightly and looked through her tears into the reflection of the window in front of her. Behind her stood three Praetorians. One stepped toward her, pistol in hand.

Her vision focused and her muscles tightened, a clarity she had never felt before washing over her.

"The ProConsul sends her regards to you and your father," mocked the Praetorian as Martin felt the hard metal of the pistol's barrel against the back of her head.

In the blink of an eye it was over.

Martin spun to her left, simultaneously deflecting the Praetorian's pistol as it fired and removing her would-be assassin's head with her sword. Her movement carried her toward the second Praetorian, whom she impaled against the wall. Martin's path was set. Ignoring the pain from a round that had torn into her arm, she again pivoted and stepped toward the last attacker. Grasping the Praetorian's gun hand, she twisted his weapon toward the floor. She drew her pistol, placed the barrel under his chin, and fired.

The sound of gunfire faded and was replaced by the moans of the Praetorian pinned to the wall by Martin's sword.

She slowly turned and holstered her pistol as she walked over to the impaled Praetorian.

As she neared him, he reached for his pistol.

Martin mechanically grabbed his right hand and extended his arm parallel to the floor.

Staring into the man's eyes, she drew one of the knives from her vest and drove it into the Praetorian's right hand.

He let out a scream. "You will rot in Capro, traitor!" he spat, blood filling his mouth.

"Where is Astra Varus?" she asked.

"Traitor," he replied, spitting blood into her face.

Keeping her gaze locked on the Praetorian, she grabbed his other hand and another knife.

"Where?"

"Bitch!"

And she drove the second knife into his left hand.

"Next I will start taking pieces," she whispered into his ear.

The Praetorian let out two heavy breaths against the pain and his impeding betrayal.

"The Forum," he mumbled.

Martin turned and walked toward the body of the constable her father had killed.

"Let me go or finish this!" demanded the Praetorian.

She leaned down and withdrew her father's sword from the constable's body and turned back toward the guard.

"Do it!" he shouted.

Martin ignored the dying Praetorian as she examined her father's sword. Her father had held this sword when he swore to defend the ProConsul with his life. Now she would use it to take the life of Astra Varus.

She slowly looked up toward the Praetorian.

"The Praetorians will bleed today like they have never bled before," she promised. "And then I will use this Praetorian sword to take the life of your precious ProConsul."

"You —"

The Praetorian's response abruptly ended as Martin drove her father's sword into his throat.

Chapter 19

Brilliant flashes of blue rippled across the darkness of space as Akota warships completed their jumps into Humani territory. In the Combat Information Center of Admiral Whitehorse's flagship, *Winterfall*, Stone stood anxiously as the tactical screen updated to show his home planet, Alpha Humana.

"Status," barked Admiral Whitehorse.

"Standby, Sir," replied the Fleet Tactical Officer, her 3-D tactical plot flashing with contacts. "All units accounted for with the exception of the frigate *Rabbit* and the battleship *Yellow Horse*."

"Have they reported?"

"Incoming electron spin message from *Yellow Horse* … jump coordinate computer is down… estimate one hour for repairs. Nothing from *Rabbit*, Sir."

"Damn it," cursed Whitehorse. "Very well, Commander."

Whitehorse turned toward Stone, still staring at the tactical plot.

"Are you okay, Marshal?"

"Oh … yes, Admiral," replied Stone, refocusing himself. "If you would have told me three years ago that I would be standing on the bridge of a Terillian warship leading an invasion of my home planet —"

"Fate is a funny thing — and we're all at her mercy."

"She's more like an evil bitch with a cruel sense of humor."

"Maybe so," chuckled Whitehorse. "But either way, she has put you here. Are you ready?"

"All troops are loaded into dropships and transports. We'll be ready when the launch call comes."

"Well that —"

"Contacts!" interrupted the FTO.

"Number and type," ordered Whitehorse.

"Multiple … twenty-five Hanmani orbital destroyers and … nine battlecruisers with several dozen escorts."

"That will be part of the home fleet. The rest must be at the Gateway Station."

"Scan for Akota identification codes," ordered Whitehorse, turning toward Stone. "If your agent succeeded, they should be flashing friendly electronic idents."

"Nothing, Sir."

"Damn it," replied Stone. "But it doesn't mean the plan isn't still working."

"True, but I would feel a lot better if they were flashing the right codes," replied Whitehorse. "FTO, pass the word to all units — Weapons Tight, Condition Red."

"Time for me to join my troops," said Stone. "Good luck, Admiral."

"Good luck, Mar —"

"Multiple neutrino spikes," reported the FTO.

"Where?" asked Whitehorse.

"Grids 7-Alpha, 7-Bravo, 3-Delta, and 3-Charlie. Twenty-five signatures in total."

"Idents?"

"They're …" The FTO turned toward Admiral Whitehorse. "They're Doran ships, Sir."

"Dorans?" replied Whitehorse.

"Yes, Sir. Twenty-three orbital destroyers and ten battlecruisers … multiple escorts …" The upper-right corner of the FTO's screen began to flash red. "Targeting scan being run, Sir. Picking up fighters inbound."

"Damn it," cursed Whitehorse. "To all units, Weapons Free."

"Can we get through?" asked Stone.

"Maybe, but it will cost us," replied Whitehorse. "It appears our plan is already starting to come apart."

"Maybe," replied Stone. "But we haven't heard from the other elements."

"Comms, do we have any reports from Task Force Scout or Raven?"

The fleet communications officer turned toward Whitehorse.

"Task Force Scout reports attack underway. They have confirmed some Hanmani ships are supporting, but are tied up fighting amongst themselves. Task Force Raven reports attack underway … no other reports."

"Well, at least part of the plan seems to be working," said Whitehorse.

"Can you get my troops into high orbit, Admiral?" asked Stone.

"I'll try to punch a hole through with the battleships and provide cover for your landing. But we'll have to be quick so I can get my carriers back into the fight. Without them, we could lose the fleet, and I don't think you want to be on the surface without a fleet providing cover."

Stone's memory flashed to the molten boulders of metal raining down on Juliet 3. If the fleet was lost, the Humani and Doral orbital destroyers would vaporize the landing zones from orbit before the assault could even get off the ground. "No, I don't."

"FTO, order the diversion force, the Scout Rangers, and their fighter cover to launch. They need to take out as many of those orbital destroyers as they can."

"Aye, Sir," replied the FTO.

Stone's thoughts flashed to Mori as he heard the order for her teams to launch passed over the circuit. Part of him wished he had turned down command so he could be with her at that moment. But he couldn't think of that now. "I'll be awaiting the launch order, Admiral," he said, turning toward the exit.

"I'll get you into orbit and launched, Marshal," replied Whitehorse. "It's up to you after that."

***

Inside the Forum communications center, two officers frantically tracked dozens of incoming messages.

"What the hell is going on, Captain?" asked a young lieutenant.

"The Gateway Station has just gone to full alert, and Home Fleet command is reporting a Terillian attack on the Station," replied the captain.

"I just received a report from the battlecruiser *Tali Drax* and the orbital destroyer *Raptor* ... they are reporting mutinies and fighting amongst the crew." The lieutenant paused as he read another message burst. "*Meridi IV* reports being attacked by *Seria Vatri.*"

"This doesn't make sense."

"No," gasped the lieutenant.

"What is it?"

"Terillian ships have been reported in striking distance of Alpha Humana! This can't be happening. What are we supposed to be doing with this information?"

"I —" The captain paused. "High Command has just issued a shelter warning for the entire planet."

"We need to contact Colonel Maxia and —"

A buzz on their console alerted them that someone was at the entrance to the center.

The lieutenant activated the door camera.

"It's a Praetorian," he said.

"Well, open it," ordered the captain. "He might know what's going on."

As the door slid open, the body of the Praetorian fell forward onto the floor. Standing behind him was Martin, sword in hand. The captain glanced toward one of his data screens, flashing the arrest warrant for Martin.

"You!" he shouted as he reached for his pistol.

***

Martin lunged forward, driving her sword into the captain's chest as she crashed her left boot into the lieutenant's knee. As the lieutenant fell to the floor, Martin yanked the sword from the captain's chest and laid the lieutenant's chest open with a powerful slash.

Catching her breath, Martin set her sword on the console.

Pulling up the priority message page, she punched in ALPHA: FE 2S-4, 3S-21, 4S-3, BRAVO: PH 3S-1, 3P-1, and XE 4D-4, 5S-2, and 5P-4 for the Akota fleet valance sequence. In the message block, she typed: LANDING FORCE CHARLIE OSCAR FRM GYM CHAMP BK ABORT ABORT ABORT END MSG.

She activated the ENCRYPT key and pressed SEND before grabbing her sword.

"Now for you, Astra Varus."

***

"How long until we launch, Sir?" asked an anxious lieutenant.

"Not much longer, Lieutenant," replied Stone, standing by the command center in his dropship.

As he waited for the word to launch, he listened on the tactical circuits as the battle unfolded. Through the chaotic chatter he heard Mori's voice.

Command, Sierra Romeo Alpha Team, breach of targets Heavy 002, 003, 006, 009, 010, 012 complete.

He wanted so badly to be there.

"Sir," interrupted General Vae.

"Yes, General? Is it the launch order?"

"No, Sir. Admiral Whitehorse requests your presence in CIC immediately."

"Why?"

"He didn't say, Marshal."

"Damn it," cursed Stone. "Stay ready for the launch order."

***

Stone slowed from a sprint as he reached the ballistic doors of *Winterfall's* CIC. *"THIS IS THE TAO … INCOMING ENEMY AIRCRAFT … ALL AIR DEFENSE SQUADRONS LAUNCH,"* echoed through the ship's announcing system as he stopped in front of two guards posted at the entrance to CIC.

"Marshal Stone for Admiral Whitehorse," said Stone.

The guards moved aside and Stone stepped inside as the ballistic doors slowly opened. He was met immediately by Whitehorse.

"We just received this via electron spin," he said, handing Stone the printout of a report.

Stone quickly scanned over the message Martin had sent from the Forum communications center. "When did this —"

"I called for you as soon as we received it. Task Force Scout is heavily engaged and we haven't heard from Raven since the initial report. And now this. Is this from your contact?"

"Damn it. Yes, it's her," replied Stone. "The plan must be compromised." He looked up toward Whitehorse. "We have to abort the attack."

"Son of a bitch," cursed Whitehorse. "We were so close," he added, looking at Alpha Humana through the viewing screen. "FTO!" he shouted … "To all units, Fallen Eagle, Fallen Eagle; commence combat recovery of all fighters and attack craft. Send word to Task Force Scout and Raven as well as to Akota command. Task Force Eagle is aborting the landing."

"Aye, Sir," acknowledged the FTO.

"How long will it take to get everyone back?" asked Stone.

"Air Combat?" asked Whitehorse. "How long until recovery?"

"Should be about fifteen minutes for air defense and attack craft, Sir. Word has been passed for the Scout Rangers to break off their attacks … awaiting reply."

"Admiral, receiving flash message from Task Force Scout," interrupted the FTO. "Hanmani fleet has been reinforced by Doran warships. They're breaking off the attack, but report Gateway Station has been destroyed."

"Destroyed?" asked Stone.

"Yes, Marshal," replied the FTO. "Admiral Willow reports one of their own battlecruisers rammed into it."

"Plaxis," said Stone. "He must have realized it was falling apart and did what he had to in order to takeout the station."

"At least part of the attack has been successful," said Whitehorse.

"Admiral, Scout Rangers report all units embarking except track Heavy 006. That's team Alpha One," reported the FTO.

"Alpha One? That's Ka-itsenko Ino'ka's team."

"Ino'ka? Have they made any reports?"

The FTO looked toward the Admiral.

"Tell me!" shouted Stone.

"Yes, Marshal," replied the FTO. "They reported they had taken out the ship's jump and main battery reactors but were cut off from their dropships."

"Patch me into their circuit," said Stone.

The FTO again looked toward Admiral Whitehorse.

"Do it," ordered Whitehorse.

"Aye, Sir," replied the FTO. "Patching in now," she added, reaching a headset to Stone.

Stone grabbed the headset. "Alpha One, this is Landing Force Actual, over? Alpha One, this is Landing Force Actual … Ino'ka, this is Magakisca."

The circuit cracked as Mori's voice could be heard over gunfire through the circuit.

"Magakisca, what's happened?"

"I don't know. But Martin sent a warning to abort."

"Damn it —" A burst of automatic fire flooded the circuit. "They blocked off our path to the dropship. We tried to punch through but there are too many."

"How many casualties?"

"I'm down to twelve with five wounded."

"Where are you?"

"Standby … Frame two hundred, port side … fifth deck."

"Hangar Bay Bravo is about thirty frames aft of your position and up one deck. Can you make it there?"

Gunshots echoed through the communications circuit.

"Do we have another option?" answered Mori.

"No," replied Stone. "Just get there … and I'll get to you."

"But the withdraw —"

"Just get there, Ino'ka."

Stone looked toward Whitehorse. "I need one of your transports and fifteen minutes."

"I'll give you as long as I can, Marshal."

***

Stone raced through the hangar bay toward his dropship. The two minutes it had taken him to get there were two he couldn't afford to lose. Just as his ship came into sight, Stone glanced to his right at battle-damaged fighter billowing smoke. As teams moved in to extinguish the flames, the pilot jumped from the cockpit.

It was Orion.

"Stone," she shouted, seeing him. "What the fuck happened?"

Stone stopped. "Mori's trapped on one of the orbital destroyers. I have to get —"

"How?"

"I'm taking my dropship over."

"You'll need cover."

"Your ship is damaged and I don't have time … I have to go," he replied as he started toward his ship again.

"Don't worry, I'll catch up," shouted Orion as Stone sprinted away.

In a few seconds, Stone reached his ship and quickly made his way to the command module.

"Sir, why was the abort order given?" asked Vae.

"I don't have time to explain right now," he replied, activating the ship's intercom and speaking. "This is Marshal Stone. The attack has been aborted but I intend to board an orbital destroyer to save some of our Akota brother warriors. This mission may be a one-way trip, so this is volunteer only. You have thirty seconds to exit the ship if you are not coming."

Stone stood silent. No one moved.

"We're awaiting your orders, Sir," replied Vae.

"Very well, General. Prepare to launch."

Chapter 20

Stone stood by the pilot of his dropship as it exited the hangar bay, his focus centered on the tactical plot.

"There," he said, "track Heavy 006. That's our target."

"Yes, Sir," replied the pilot. "But …"

"What is it, Lieutenant?"

"I'm picking up multiple fighters around that vessel, and our scans show most of their air defense systems are still operational. We'll never make it —"

"Dropship 1A, this is Raven Group leader in Foxtrot 7 Sierra. I'll make a path … you keep up."

Stone looked through the cockpit to see a foxtrot fighter drift into position directly ahead of his ship.

"Let's go," ordered Orion, the two ships accelerating toward the orbital destroyer.

"1A, Raven leader, keep tight on your track. I'm gonna have to maneuver to clear the path, but you stay true."

"Roger, Raven leader," replied the dropship pilot.

Stone watched through the cockpit as Orion banked hard right and continued to accelerate as two Doran fighters bore down on their positions. A blast from her guns obliterated the first fighter as she rolled left and down, only to pull into a vertical ascent and roll back onto the second fighter. Before it could turn to face her, another blast tore off its wing.

"Who the hell is that pilot, Sir?" asked the dropship pilot.

"Just an old smuggler, Lieutenant," replied Stone with a smile.

Suddenly, Stone was almost knocked off his feet as a Humani fighter cut in from their left and raked the side of his ship with strafing run.

"Dropship 1A taking evasive act —"

"Negative 1A, stay on course. I got —"

Stone saw the Humani fighter disintegrate into a dozen pieces.

"— got it," continued Orion. *"You're clear of aircraft. I'm gonna make a pass over the hangar entrance to draw the self-defense guns."*

Stone watched as Orion again accelerated and banked right then swung left and flashed past the hangar bay entrance, her ship followed by tracers and bursts from the ship's defense systems.

Suddenly the dropship rocked to port as one of the orbital destroyer's defense batteries tore into the starboard side.

"Hold on, Sir," warned the pilot.

Stone gripped the back of the pilot's seat as the ship soared sideways through the air boundary to the hangar bay.

"Shifting thrusters!" shouted the pilot, the ship jerking forward and to the right before slamming onto the deck of the hangar bay.

Stone crashed into the control panel between the pilot and navigator and rolled onto the deck.

"Are you okay, Sir?" asked the pilot as alarms and sirens blared.

"Fine," grumbled Stone, hiding the pain shooting through his shoulder.

Pushing himself off the floor, Stone rushed into the command room. As he entered, he saw General Vae assisting a soldier with an injured arm. "Is everyone okay?" he asked.

"Yes, Sir," replied Captain Juli.

The acrid odor of overheated and burning electronics filled Stone's senses. Looking behind Juli, he saw smoke drifting from an electrical panel. "We need to get off this ship."

"Yes, Sir," replied Vae. "Captain Juli, disembark and set up a perimeter."

"Yes, Sir," said Juli, turning toward his small squad. "Let's move!"

"Follow me!" shouted Stone, Mori the only thought on his mind.

The dropship doors flew open and Stone burst into the hangar toward a stack of containers, bullets filling the air around him. "Ino'ka, where are you?" he shouted into his comms circuit.

"*Forward starboard corner*," came her answer.

"We're aft, starboard."

"*Yeah, that landing was hard to miss.*"

"Can you make it to us?"

"*We're on the way if you can provide cover.*"

Stone's attention shifted to a Terillian fighter as it shot into the hangar, its rear section on fire. The fighter, still airborne, came to a sudden stop and turned toward the forward section of the hangar bay.

"*Alpha Team leader, this is Raven leader. Get your heads down. I'll clear a path*," came Orion's voice over the circuit as small arms fire ricocheted off her burning fighter.

"Roger Ra —"

Mori's reply was drowned out as Orion's guns opened fire inside the hangar. In seconds, the path between Mori's and Stone's position was strewn with wrecked aircraft and bodies of Humani crewmembers and troops.

"You're clear," reported Orion, as her fighter's engines failed and the ship dropped five meters onto the deck with a metallic clang.

"Raven leader, Alpha Team leader. Report status."

"*Alive*," grunted Orion over the circuit. "*I'm coming to you.*"

The forward section of the hangar bay cleared of most Humani, Stone's team laid down covering fire against the few remaining troops left in the area as Mori's team raced over the wreckage caused by Orion. The remaining Scout Rangers sprinted across the hangar, some carrying wounded comrades. Through the chaos, Stone's focus was fixed on Mori. In the rear of the group, she stopped every few meters to return covering fire for her troops.

As they raced toward Stone's group, one of the Rangers took a round to the leg and fell to the deck.

"Keep moving!" Stone heard Mori shout to her men as she ran toward the wounded Ranger.

"Cover her!" shouted Stone.

Mori stopped at the wounded Ranger, quickly turning to topple an advancing Humani soldier with a burst from her rifle. She grabbed the Ranger's arm and helped him to his feet. Throwing the wounded man's arm over her shoulder, Mori began to help the man hobble toward safety. A few meters from cover, she looked up toward Stone. Her green eyes locked onto his gaze and she smiled.

Stone returned her smile but suddenly his eyes opened wide. "No!" he yelled as he saw a grenade land next to her. "Grenade!"

Mori's expression changed just before the grenade detonated, enveloping Mori and the other Ranger. From the explosion, he saw her body twist and go airborne from the force of the explosion.

Stone rushed from his position, ignoring the gunfire.

"Protect the Marshal!" yelled Captain Juli, and several Humani soldiers leapt from their positions to follow Stone.

Bullets whizzed past Stone as he sprinted toward Mori. Nearing her, Stone saw her start to crawl toward the other Ranger. His already pounding heart felt like it would explode when he saw a trail of blood from her body leading back to the lower part of her left leg.

He reached her just as she made it to the other Ranger.

"Ino'ka!" he shouted, taking her into his arms and lifting her off the ground.

"The Ranger —"

"He's gone," replied Stone, glancing at the pile of meat and bones that used to be the Ranger.

He looked into her green eyes, now dull and heavy. "I'll get you out of here."

Covered by his men and the others, he cradled Mori in his arms and ran back toward cover.

"How is she?" asked Orion when Stone reached cover and laid her on the ground.

"Get me a med-pack!" he shouted, looking over her injuries.

Blood was pumping from the mangled left leg, her calf and foot gone. He could also see blood seeping through the shirt of her uniform. He grabbed her shirt and ripped it open to see her undershirt soaked. Stone lifted her undershirt. Blood oozed through four wounds on the left side of her stomach.

"My men," coughed Mori. "Did —"

"Don't worry," interrupted Stone. "Get me some damn meds!" he ordered.

"Here, Sir," replied Captain Juli, handing Stone a med-pack.

Stone grabbed the pack from Juli and frantically searched for coagulate gel. Finding it, he pulled it from the pack.

"That won't be enough," said Orion. "We'll need to apply a tourniquet."

"Here," replied Stone, reaching the gel applicator out to Orion. "Put this on her stomach wounds first."

Orion began applying the blood-clotting agent and Stone took a black band from the pack and slid it over the bloody stump of Mori's leg. Once around her leg, he depressed a small red button and the band began to tighten until the pumping of blood from Mori's leg slowed to a small trickle.

"Magakisca," moaned Mori.

"Yes," he replied, almost frantic.

"Maybe my dreams were wrong," she laughed weakly. "Maybe I will see the Great Spirit today."

"You're not going to die today," grunted Stone. He placed his hand, now covered in Mori's blood, on her painted face. "I'm not gonna let you."

"Marshal," interrupted Captain Juli. "We need to get out of here."

"Just wait!" yelled Stone, his gaze still locked on Mori. "Orion?"

"The gel is applied," she answered. "I'm attaching a fluid inducer and platelet pack to her arm." Orion looked up toward Stone. "And your captain's right. We need to get off this ship."

Finally breaking his focus on Mori, Stone looked around. Only a few of the Rangers were left uninjured and several of his own men had been wounded. He glanced over the cover to see Humani troops moving to flank them. Looking behind him, he saw the burning hulk of Orion's fighter and his wrecked dropship. But beyond, he saw a Humani Eagle bomber.

"Lieutenant, can you fly that?" he said to his pilot.

"I don't know, Sir. It —"

"I got it," interrupted Orion, who had joined the group. "If it flies, I can fly it. Will everyone fit?"

"We'll have to," he replied. "Everyone move toward that bomber!" he ordered.

Stone took Mori into his arms and prepared to stand. "Move," he ordered, and the group burst from cover for the bomber.

Stone and the others raced across the hangar bay to the bomber.

"Use the dropship for cover and protect our flanks!" ordered General Vae as Orion opened the access to the bomber.

"You two," said Orion to the pilot and the navigator, "come with me to the cockpit and help me get this thing off the ground … General Vae, you too." She turned toward Stone. "You've got to get everyone else squeezed into the electronics bay and the payload compartment."

Stone, Mori still in his arms, ascended the small ladder and gently carried her through the already cramped electronics bay and into the payload compartment. Laying her on the deck, he ran his hand over her head. "It's going —"

She had stopped breathing.

"Juli, get me the shock pads," he yelled. "No! You can't die," he pleaded.

"Here, Sir," said Juli.

"Get another fluid and platelet pack in her," ordered Stone, grabbing the two small cylinders from Juli. He pressed them to Mori's chest and side, waited until the lights on the device turned green, and depressed a button on each, sending a shock through Mori's body.

Mori's body jerked violently. He read the readout on the cylinder: INEFFECTIVE TRY AGAIN. "Shit," he cursed, his hands shaking.

"Fluids and platelets are attached, Sir," replied Juli.

The green light appeared again and Stone depressed the button. Mori's body contorted and she let out a grunt. He looked at the readout again: NORMAL RHYTHM DO NOT SHOCK.

Stone dropped the cylinders onto the deck and put his hand on Mori's forehead. "You're gonna make it … you have to."

"*Standby for takeoff,*" came over the intercom. "*It's time to get the hell out of here.*"

***

Standing on the bridge of *Winterfall*, Admiral Whitehorse watched as flashes of blue indicated the Akota warships were beginning to jump.

"Are all fighters accounted for?" asked Whitehorse.

"Yes, Sir," replied the ship's commanding officer.

"FTO, do we have a status from the other task forces?"

"Task Force Scout reports the destruction of the Gateway Station. Admiral Willow reports the loss of one carrier and four battleships. Task

Force Raven reported they were able to start the attack, but multiple Humani warships jumped into the area about thirty minutes in. Admiral Evergreen reports the loss of two carriers and five battleships and was not able to perform a damage assessment before they jumped."

"How many did we lose?" asked Whitehorse.

"We lost seven carriers and eight battleships … over eighty thousand men, at least."

"Damn it," cursed Whitehorse. "And Marshal Stone?"

"Recovered, Sir. Ka-itsenko Ino'ka is badly wounded."

"This has been a very bad day," replied Whitehorse, turning toward *Winterfall's* commanding officer. "Captain Rain, you have permission to jump."

***

"Are these the last of them?" asked Astra Varus, slowly walking in front of five First Family patriarchs on their knees in front of her onboard her private corvette, *Dominotra*.

"All that we know of right now, ProConsul," reported General Vispa. "It appears a few escaped, and I am sure we will find more as the interrogations begin."

"And Martin's teams?"

"Orders are out and reports are in that all of them have been dealt with except for the Marine.

Apparently he took out the mercs assigned to kill him and disappeared into the Port Royal polis."

"The other are …"

"Dead," replied Vispa.

"Put bounties of one million credits on the heads of everyone that escaped — dead or alive," ordered Astra.

Astra stopped in front of Senator Marcus Tyris.

"Senator Tyris," said Astra, reaching down and running her hand across his cheek. "It seems your little coup has failed."

"We cannot live under the yoke of the Xen forever, ProConsul," he replied. "One day the Humani people must regain their freedom."

"You are partially right, Senator," said Astra with a smile. "One day we will be free of the Xen. But the Humani people will always need to be led by a powerful leader — a leader that will not only shake off the Xen, but make them serve us."

"You're insane," replied Tyris.

"I am not the one on my knees, Senator." Astra turned toward General Vispa. "You have reported on her team, General, but any word on that bitch, Martin?"

"No, ProConsul. The last report was from the teams that responded to her father's facility."

"How fucking hard is it to kill one person?" huffed Astra. As she spoke, she pulled Vispa's pistol, turned, and fired point-blank into Senator Tyris's forehead. "See? … dead."

"But ProConsul —"

Astra turned back toward Vispa, the pistol pointed toward its owner. "Now, General Vispa, you were not about to give me an excuse, were you?"

"No, ProConsul. We will find her."

"See that you do … I do not want that bitch running free on my planet."

She turned back toward the remaining traitors. Glancing at the body of Tyris as blood flowed from his head onto the deck, she spoke. "Now for the rest of these traitorous swine," she spat. "General Vispa, transport them to Capro and keep them alive until they talk … but just barely alive."

"Yes, ProConsul," replied Vispa. "Guards, take this trash away."

"And throw Senator Tyris in the cell with them," added Astra.

As the guards drug away the remaining prisoners — and Tyris's body — Vispa turned toward Astra.

"Your cousin has already started arresting anyone linked with the traitors. We will find them all."

"They all go to Capro," replied Astra. "But once they have talked, including those four that just left, I want them returned to Alpha Humana for public crucifixion."

"Yes, ProConsul."

"Now, General, what is the status of the battle?"

"The attack on Alpha Humana has been stopped with several Terillian capital ships lost, although we did lose the Gateway Station."

"It is gone?"

"Yes, ProConsul," replied Vispa. "Admiral Plaxis's flagship rammed it. Several mutinies have been reported among Home Fleet ships, but most have been put down. The few remaining ships are under attack by loyal forces. There have been uprisings in six regions — Lunari Fields, Juli, Vae, Fortress Malius, Centius Plains, and the Tri-Cities. The resistance has been crushed in all areas except the Lunari Fields and Vae regions. We are mobilizing additional forces against those regions, and they should soon be under control."

"Show them no mercy, General. If the resistance lasts more than a week, you are authorized to conduct orbital bombardment."

"Of our own planet?" Vispa paused. "Yes, of course, ProConsul."

"And I want all families believed to be involved in this rebellion stripped of First Family status. Except for the Malius family. Targus Malius will be elevated to Patriarch by order of the ProConsul for his service to the Republic."

"Yes, ProConsul, but isn't he dead?"

"The people will hear there is a reward for service to the Republic. His death will be reported later as act of an assassin."

"As you wish, ProConsul."

"And Dolus? Was there damage?"

"The base suffered significant damage in several areas, as did some of the ships under construction, but there were no major breaches. We may have been set back a few months, but the base is intact."

A red light illuminated on a nearby communications panel, indicating a priority message.

"General, find out what that is about," ordered Astra.

Vispa activated the communications panel. "This is General Vispa. What is it?"

"*Sir, this is the Communications Officer. Lord General Zorlar is en route. He wishes to have you join him and return to the Forum to discuss the battle and your plans.*"

"Of course he does," huffed Astra. "That grey-skinned bastard will expect to be even more involved in our business." She stopped to look at the pool of blood where Tyris's body had been. "And have someone clean this mess off the deck."

Astra looked up toward the overhead and exhaled. "This attempted coup nearly ruined everything. There was no word of Dolus passed over open circuits?"

"It appears not, ProConsul. The Dorans should still know nothing about Dolus."

Chapter 21

ProConsul Astra Varus stood next to Lord General Zorlar as his shuttle approached the Forum docking bay.

"The Terillians will think twice before attempting to attack us outside of the Neutral Quadrant again," smiled Astra, unconcerned with the human cost of the battle.

"You should be thankful the Emperor directed our Kings to provide this support, ProConsul," replied Zorlar. "Otherwise, you might be fighting the Terillians on the surface of your planet."

"Of course, we are thankful for the assistance from our Doran allies, General," replied Astra, veiling her disgust at acknowledging the Doran's role in winning the battle. "But do not underestimate the Humani spirit," she warned. "If they had reached the surface, they would have paid dearly … as would any invader."

"Of course," replied Zorlar in a dismissive tone.

Astra fumed but maintained her composure. It appeared Zorlar's gratitude for her public praise of his efforts had an expiration date. She let out a quick puff of air, yearning for the day she could stand over the rubble of the Xen and Doran civilizations.

The shuttle shuddered slightly, indicating it had docked. The door opened and six Praetorians stepped off the shuttle, forming for Astra's exit.

Astra approached the shuttle access and prepared to step onto the brow.

"Back inside," directed a Praetorian officer, stepping into the shuttle, his rifle at the ready.

"Report, Praetorian!" ordered Praetorian Sergeant-at-Arms Yashmiri.

"The arrival party has been attacked," reported the guard.

"How many casualties?" asked Yashmiri as he drew his sword and instinctively stood in front of Astra.

"All of them," replied the guard.

"All?"

"Yes, Praetorian Yashmiri. The entire receiving party is dead on the landing dock."

"Martin!" shouted Astra, rage exploding from her body. She stepped toward the door.

"ProConsul, please," pleaded Yashmiri. "Let us secure the landing dock and then get you to safety."

"Go!" she ordered.

More Praetorians rushed from the shuttle, weapons drawn.

"Captain," ordered Zorlar to Captain Navar. "Send five men and a mech with them."

"Aye," responded the Doran captain as he turned and quickly selected five men.

Astra watched as the Doran soldiers rushed past her, followed by the metallic thud of the weapons mech rumbling behind. She stood just inside the entrance to the shuttle, her blood boiling.

In a few moments, Yashmiri returned to Astra and Zorlar.

"ProConsul, Lord General," he reported. "The landing dock is secure, but we can't raise Forum security or any Praetorians guards assigned to the Forum. Under these circumstances I recommend we return —"

"Where is Martin?" she demanded.

"We do not know, ProConsul. We have not been able to locate her."

"Find her!" Astra fumed. "Look around you!" she added, waving her hand toward the six dead Praetorians scattered on the dock. "She is here!"

"Probably, ProConsul," replied Yashmiri. "And that is why I recommend returning to the ship."

Astra slapped Yashmiri across the face with a grunt. "Coward! I want every Praetorian in the Forum to hunt her down and —"

Astra saw Yashmiri take a slow breath, absorbing both the physical and emotional assault she had unleashed.

"ProConsul," he said slowly. "I am tasked with protecting your life … which supersedes any emotions I may feel. And I fear there are no Praetorians left in the Forum alive."

"Who is this Martin?" asked a frustrated Zorlar.

"A trained dog that has gone rabid," grumbled Astra. "She —"

She froze mid-sentence.

"Octavius!" she gasped, realizing Martin was inside the Forum somewhere. And so was her son.

"Move," she shouted as she rushed past Yashmiri.

Octavius was the only thought on Astra's mind as she ran toward the entrance to the Forum. Near the door, she heard Yashmiri's voice.

"Secure a path for the ProConsul! Move ahead!"

Astra saw three Praetorians and two Doran guards rush past her through the door as the large mech took station just outside.

Suddenly, a wave of pressure and heat lifted Astra off her feet, knocking her to the ground, an explosion rocking the landing dock. Her bones ached and debris fell onto her body as she lay on her back, looking up at the Humani sky. A high-pitched tone echoed through her head as she struggled to take in air.

Yashmiri knelt beside her, his right arm badly mangled. He was shouting, but the ringing in her ears prevented her from hearing him. She looked to her left and saw the lifeless body of Lord General Zorlar lying next to her, his pale blue eyes frozen in death.

"ProConsul! ProConsul!"

As if a switch was flipped, her hearing cleared.

"ProConsul! The door was wired. You must return to the ship!" reported Yashmiri.

Her thoughts shot back toward Octavius. "My son!" she yelled, shaking off the effects from the explosion. She scrambled to her feet and again headed toward the entrance, now strewn with wrecked bodies of Praetorians and Doran warriors. Without stopping, she rushed past the bodies and the burning hulk of the mech into the hallway leading to her private chambers.

A few meters from the entrance to the Senatorial subcommittee hall, she saw three

Praetorians sprawled on the floor in pools of blood. Next to them was Senator Knoxus, trying to apply pressure to a gunshot wound in his leg. She glanced toward the Senator, who made eye contact with her.

"She killed them all!" shouted the Senator.

Astra ignored the Senator, grabbing a pistol from one of the dead Praetorians and continuing down the passageway.

Her heart sank as she turned the corner to her private complex. "No," she groaned, looking on the bodies of two Praetorians at the entrance to her chambers. Anxiety and rage filled her mind as she readied her pistol and rushed into the room.

The scene took her breath.

Two more Praetorians lay just inside the room, their bodies riddled with bullets. Another was crumpled onto a chair with his chest torn open by a sword.

Astra heard a noise and spun to her left to see one of her servants tied to a column, struggling to free herself. She rushed to the servant and pulled the gag from her mouth.

"Where is Octavius?" she yelled.

"Paladin Martin," panted the servant. "She killed the Praetorians and —"

Astra slapped the frightened servant. "Octavius! Where is he?"

"I don't know," answered the frightened servant. "Two Praetorians and Mr. Artemis rushed into the room … these three came in after … then Paladin Martin…she killed them and —"

"What did you do?" demanded Astra.

"I tried —"

"Not hard enough," growled Astra through her teeth, placing the pistol to the servant's head and firing.

Stepping away from the limp body of the servant, Astra walked toward Octavius's room. She wanted to run but could only walk, afraid of what she would see. Her heart pounded as if it would explode when she opened the door.

Another dead Praetorian. She involuntarily began to shake, her breath growing heavy as she frantically scanned the room.

"Octavius!" she called out, but her voice had grown weak from anxiety.

She let out a gasp when she saw the overturned crib.

She rushed to it.

Beside the crib were the bodies of the Praetorian guards and her spy Artemis. An old Praetorian sword protruded from Artemis's chest.

Astra grew dizzy as she knelt down and rolled Artemis onto his back. As the limp body flopped over, she saw a note stuck his chest by the blade.

Her breath left her body as she read it:

THE MOST DANGEROUS ANIMAL IS A TRAINED DOG TURNING ON A

CRUEL MASTER — YOU TOOK MY FATHER SO I TOOK YOUR SON — COME GET ME BITCH

Astra let out a scream that echoed through the chamber and down the bloody hallways of the Forum.

***

Martin grimaced slightly, looking down at her wounded left arm. She reached for another neuro-med but paused; she would need to remain focused.

Martin leaned over to the navigator panel and punched in a set of coordinates. With the fleet still recovering from the chaos of battle, Martin knew a single hawk attack craft would go undetected. She drew in a deep breath as she pushed the accelerator forward.

Clearing the atmosphere of Alpha Humana, she saw the carnage from the battle. Doran and Humani escorts and fighters darted in all directions between hulks of capital ships destroyed in the fight. She could see escape pods being jettisoned from a Terillian battleship, hundreds of little flashes of light followed by tiny streaks as the pods accelerated away from the ship.

Looking on, she saw several Doran and Humani fighters change course toward the damaged battleship. "No!" she shouted aloud as the fighters began opening fire on the escape pods.

She wanted to help, to save even one, but she couldn't. Her cargo was too important.

Her eyes widened as she saw three bright lines trace across the space in front of her from a Doran orbital destroyer. She could only watch as the superheated balls of metal plasma slammed into the damaged battleship, splitting it in two.

"Time to get out of here," she said aloud, continuing to accelerate the ship toward the darkness of space.

Clear of the battlefield, Martin collapsed back into the pilot's chair as the events of the day washed over her. The Praetorians would long remember this day … if only Astra Varus had been there. A noise from a small bundle in the navigator seat drew her attention.

"Don't worry, little one," she said. "It's time to meet your father."

Chapter 22

Stone stood by Mori's hospital bed with General Vae standing next to him, a data pad in his hand.

"Are you sure you don't want to discuss this later, Marshal Stone?" asked General Vae.

"I need to get an update, General," replied Stone, staring at the unconscious Mori. "I just don't want to leave her right now."

"I understand, Sir. Shall I begin?"

"Yes, General."

"Overall casualties to the invasion force was 21,354 of the 203,345 embarked. Of the 21,354, there were 15,345 killed, four thousand seven hundred eight-three wounded, and one thousand two hundred twenty-six missing. Most were lost with the orbital destroyers and carriers that were destroyed. The casualty list includes four generals, fifteen colonels —"

"Prepare a schedule for me visit each of the wounded, General. And start with the enlisted."

"Yes, Sir, but as they are split up amongst many ships in the fleet, it may take several days to see them all."

"Just make the schedule, General," said Stone, looking up toward Vae.

"Of course, Sir."

"Have we heard anything from Alpha Humana or the Home Fleet?"

"Nothing, Sir."

"Then Astra has tightened the vise," replied Stone. "That will be all for now, General," he continued, looking back at Mori.

"Yes, Sir." Vae paused. "And, Sir …"

"What is it, General?"

"She fought bravely."

"Thank you, General."

"Shall I meet you here again tomorrow, Sir?"

"Yes, General. Do try to get some sleep."

As General Vae walked away, Stone returned his focus to Mori. He sat with his head in his palm and his other gripping hers. Exhausted, he soon fell asleep.

The binging of medical equipment startled Stone back to consciousness.

"Are you the new doctor?" asked Stone.

"I am Colonel Stormrace, Marshal Stone," replied the man. "I've come over from the carrier *Yellow Moon* at Admiral Winter's request."

"Thank you. Has there been any change?" he asked with the same desperation in his voice as every other conversation he'd had with doctors and nurses for the past week.

"Sorry, Marshal," replied the doctor. "Her condition remains stable but unchanged."

Stone turned back toward Mori as he awaited the doctor's response. She had a oxygen mask over her mouth; Stone could just barely make out the air tube protruding from her throat and forcing oxygen into her lungs. He looked down to the maze of tubes connected to her chest and arm. His gaze then moved down to the large cylinder where her lower leg should be. "Will the chamber work?"

"It should, Marshal," replied the doctor. "The regeneration chambers are usually very successful. The problem is —"

"The loss of oxygen," interrupted Stone. He had heard the same explanation from every doctor he had asked.

"I see you have met Colonel Stormrace," said *Winterfall*'s Chief Medical Officer, Commander Ravenheart, as he joined the two men. "He is the senior medical officer in the fleet."

"Yes, Commander. We were discussing the oxygen issue."

"Yes, Dr. Ravenheart," added Stormrace, "I understand you had to resuscitate her several times the first day?"

"We had to bring her back once getting back to *Winterfall*," said Stone.

"And the doctors here lost her three more times the first day," added Ravenheart. "The other doctors fear, and I concur, that she may have suffered some damage to her brain due to momentary shortfall of oxygen during the arrests."

"When will you know?" he asked.

"Several weeks, Sir. We need to keep her sedated and on forced oxygen for a while. It will help the regeneration process and is also precautionary for her possible brain injury. We have also introduced nano-neuron recovery cells into her blood stream. It is newer technology, but has shown promise." Stormrace placed his hand on Stone's shoulder. "We are doing everything we can."

"Thank you, Colonel," replied Stone. "She's …" He took a deep breath to compose himself. "She's important to me."

"She's important to all of us, Marshal," replied Stormrace.

He turned back toward Mori, placing his hand on her arm. "She's everything to —"

A commotion outside of Mori's room drew Stone's attention.

"You can't go in there," he heard on the other side of the thin door.

"Stop me," replied a familiar voice.

"Emily," declared Stone, standing and facing the door.

The door slowly opened and he saw the familiar red hair, tied tight in a ponytail, enter the room.

"Emi —"

His attention quickly shifted to a bundle in her arms. He looked closer and saw a tiny hand.

"Sir," said Martin, a mixture of anguish and relief on her face.

"What is —"

"Allow me to introduce you to your son, Octavius."

Stone's knees weakened. The son he thought he would never see — one he thought would grow learning to hate him — was right in front of him.

"It's really —"

"Here, Sir," said Martin with a smile as she placed Octavius in Stone's arms. "I couldn't give you Alpha Humana, but I can give you your son."

Stone took Octavius in his trembling arms, looking into his son's eyes for the first time.

"Astra?" he asked, looking up toward Martin.

"I couldn't get to her," grumbled Martin. "But the Praetorians will never be the same."

"How did it fall apart?"

"I don't know, Sir." Martin looked past Stone toward Mori. "Is she gonna make it?"

He looked up at Martin, tears flowing from the emotional avalanche of Mori's condition and holding his son in his arms for the first time. "I don't know."

"Well, she's a fighter. I know that much about her."

"Yes, she is," replied Stone.

"Where do we go from here?"

"Get back to safety, heal, and prepare for Astra Varus to unleash her rage," replied Stone.

"We'll be ready, Sir," declared Martin, placing her hand on his shoulder.

"We'd better," replied Stone as he looked down at his son. "We'd better."

About the Author

Brian Dorsey is a retired Naval Officer and is currently a Nuclear Test Engineer for a Naval Shipyard. When not spending time with his family, Brian enjoys reading and researching US and Native American history, watching good TV shows or films (anything by Joss Whedon), hunting, teaching the occasional history class, or working on his next writing project.

Current books available in the Gateway Universe

Gateway (Gateway Series Book 1)
Cold Planet (A Gateway Universe Story)
Saint (Gateway Series Book 2)
Uprising (Gateway Series Book 3)
Rise of the Wolf: Katalya's Story (A Novella)
Schism (Gateway Series Book 4)

Other MWP Books

Southern Rites
Escape of the Relentless

MWP Comics (Comic Books)

The Book of Jessica #1
The Book of Luka Graphic Novel
War Angels #1
War Angels #1.5